BETWEEN THE LIVING AND THE DEAD

SOPHIE JUPILLAT POSEY

Published by Immortal Cravings, LLC
Venice, Florida

Copyright © 2025 by Sophie Jupillat Posey
ISBN - Paperback: 979-8-9922349-0-9
ISBN - eBook : 979-8-9922349-1-6
First Edition Immortal Cravings, LLC
Library of Congress Control Number : 2024926746

Licensing Notes

Cover design by Brandi Kae Designs
Edited by C.J.

I dedicate this story to my Jupillat and Aparicio families. I also dedicate it to my darling Gma Chris and my husband Christopher Posey for their steadfast support as I search for my own origins. A huge thank you is for The Book Dragon for their support, the amazing team at Immortal Cravings, and my editors C.J. and Danita Mayer!

1

DUSK

I knew something was wrong when dusk wasn't followed by night. It was happening again; my third time this year. The sun just set over the hills, but the light froze, as if a greedy hand had seized it and squeezed it. The motes of ashen light trickled through the violet clouds into my bedroom window. I passed my hand through the dull sunbeam, my brown color paling as it mingled with the dusk. Even my gold leaf bracelet lost its luster and glow. The hoarse calling of Tia Luz Marina for dinner time quieted and softened until her always angry-sounding voice was nothing but a hush.

That time, I held still and breathed slowly, slitting my eyes until my vision doubled. *Focus on the intangible*, I coaxed myself. The withered light impregnated every corner, every detail of my messy room. It turned into ghosts the coloring books, the woolen dolls, the half-empty bottles of acrylic paint. When it fell on the spirits of my deceased friends, Niko, and Angelica, sitting on the floor by my bed, it brought them further into focus.

The queer dusk light slipped into my short bathroom hallway and vanished. I stared at that dark entryway, convinced there was something more there. For years, I'd been telling Tia Luz Marina that there were ghosts in the bathroom, but she tossed the notion aside. She said believing in ghosts was a gringa thing. Yet, when I pressed her on ghosts and gods from stories of our Peruvian culture, she shied away.

I tossed six dice to Angelica, reassured that time had frozen. The clock's hands didn't move, and I couldn't hear my Tia anymore. Like I said, that wasn't my first time. People at school talked about hormones and pimples and sex. Yet, that stuff washed over me, like Tia Luz Marina's comments that I was dishonoring our heritage. Yes, I didn't know how to speak Spanish well, I dressed like an American, and I had no idea who my parents were or the rest of the family. But I am the new generation that lives in the new world. We are without roots.

I wished I knew what had happened in the last year. Why suddenly I began seeing dead friends and people walking in the streets. The dead strangers paid me no mind. They always seemed in a rush like they had crucial business to finish. My friends flocked to me and wanted to hang out exactly like how we used to before their death. We took walks together, we played, we joked around, we read, we poked fun at stodgy looking people. I knew I wasn't crazy; the world shifted and dimmed around me every time, time pausing as if confused at the shifting reality.

I asked Angelica, "Where are you guys going tonight?"

"We're going downstairs I think," she said in her sweet, high-pitched voice.

"Yeah, we went up last time and didn't find anything cool. Besides, always going upstairs is boring," Niko said after impatiently waited his turn, eyeing his Qwixx scoresheet anxiously.

"What is upstairs and downstairs?" I asked, already knowing the answer.

"We can't tell you. Same reason you can't come with us. Yet," Angelica said, the dusk filtering into her blond hair.

Yet? That was new. But the overall message was the same. All I'd managed to infer was that upstairs and downstairs were some kind of heaven or hell. But my friends stayed mum on the topic.

"I hope downstairs will leave us alone," Niko said with a

shudder. "They weren't too nice last time. We need to be more discreet." He rolled his set of dice. Niko's checkered shirt flexed as he ticked off all his marks. His freckled face beamed at me.

I sat on my art table, pushing away the glitter pens and pots of jewelry. They were real. As real as I was. One time, we'd played a Trivial Pursuit Game, which in normal time should have taken three hours. But when my friends finally disappeared and time resumed, the penumbra around me slinking away, the clock acted like no time had passed.

I wondered how much time we'd get together this visit. I never knew how long they'd stay or when they'd come. It had all started after that terrible summer last year, when all my best friends, and all my pets had died. All for various reasons, but all had died. I had been so alone. Until I started seeing spirits. However, this sunset freezing thing was only my third time. Perhaps I would get more time as this magic event doohickey grew stronger?

I contemplated my friends. They died in a hit and run. No one had any information about who had done it. My theory was I saw my friends because they couldn't 'move on'. I wished I could help. But a selfish part of me wanted them to stay.

"Did you guys glean any info on your… upstairs and downstairs trips?" I stuttered distastefully, hating not having the specific words for those places.

I flipped through my red and black notebook entitled "Mysteries of Life." In it were the childhood nothings I'd thought had been mysteries. Neighbor's cat abducted. Teacher missing for a month. Friend's slime stolen. However, the actual solution had been easy, and in fact, only my friend's slime had been stolen by her ex-boyfriend. The rest had been dramatic conjectures of a child.

However, I hadn't lost my taste in detective stories. Everywhere I could find a mystery, I leaped with glee. But with Niko's and Angelica's hit and run, I tried to apply myself seriously. My notebook was now mostly filled with my notes about the circumstances of their death, photos of the crime scene, the extracts of police reports. Tia Luz Marina was still mad that I'd egged a friend's dad to give me copies of the documents for supposed "internship" purposes. But, it had been helpful. I managed to figure out what vehicle was used, a possible motive, and a vague sensation of a male being behind their death. Don't ask me how I knew. I knew like I knew and accepted the craziness happening around me. Some things you learn not to question.

"No," Angelica sighed mournfully, sadder that Niko was winning more than anything else.

"Nope. But we trust you," Niko said, looking up at me hopefully. "You've found secrets that no one knew about, you uncovered a thieving ring at school, you found missing pets so many times, even years after they were lost. Plus, you read Agatha Christie all the time. It's bound to rub off on you."

He was right. Those were all things I'd uncovered, yet I hadn't noted them in my book. I got up and punched him gently in the shoulder, my hand passing through.

"Speaking of Agatha Christie," I said perking up, "I've found an anthology of all her Hercule Poirot stories. It's so cool! I'm like half-way through…"

"Oh, it's time," Angelica said softly, her form dimming and vanishing.

"See you later, Cavilla," Niko shouted, waving.

They both disintegrated in the ether of the soft dusk, darkness now advancing in my room. My clock started ticking again. The tweeting of the birds resumed. And Tia Luz Marina's acrid tone belied her kind words.

"Cavillaca! Come! I made ceviche. I got fresh shrimp from the market today."

I bolted for the kitchen, my mouth watering. "What else is there?"

"Aji de Gallina," she sang bellicosely.

Even better. She'd made my favorite dishes. As I looked back wistfully at my bedroom, I pondered on my own name. Cavilla. Cavillace. Or Cavillaca. My birth certificate was illegible. My friends called me Cavilla. Tia called me Cavillaca though she hadn't always. When I was little, she called me Cavillace; stubborn as a rock, she'd say.

Even my own name was a mystery.

2

MR. JACKSON'S SEARCH

Sitting on the pier, I trailed my toes in the scummy water of the lake, watching the tiny herrings scuttle away, flashes of their distress creating minuscule bubbles. The water's warmth soothed me, as well as the bobbing of the neighbors' boats. I hoped there weren't any alligators close by, then again, I didn't really fear them.

I waited for my former clarinet professor to stop on by. Like Angelica and Niko, we couldn't predict when he would appear. He'd died five months ago perhaps from an aneurysm. His house was still being cleared out by his nieces and nephews. His boat remained at the marina, patiently waiting to be commandeered. I waited for the imperceptible flip flop of his worn-out sandals, the swish of his Hawaiian shirt, and the jingling of his shark tooth necklaces. The man was as grand a cliche as his huge smile. I missed his clarinet lessons.

Today, we had a mission. Despite his family's help in settling his affairs, he'd lost his wife's wedding ring. She died a decade prior, but he always kept her ring on a chain with him. Even when he gave lessons, that ring bobbed, nestled in his hairy chest. We tried to pinpoint a date and location of when the ring could have gone missing. Sometime before his death, he was sure. I'd scouted his old hunting grounds, the local bar, the after-school music club, his nephew's arcade. He'd gone with me of course, but no luck. Somehow, the ring had slipped off, and couldn't be found.

But I proposed that we check the lake. Every Sunday he had gone out for a solitary picnic on his boat and then a swim. There was a real possibility he had lost the ring during one of those trips. I nudged the picnic basket next to me, full of cured meats, cheese, and fruit. If he didn't come soon, I would start snacking. It didn't matter if he couldn't eat in his ghost form, etiquette was etiquette.

A swirling sensation in my limbs tugged at me. I ignored it, waiting for Mr. Jackson. When he came, I'd suggest he lead us to the middle of the lake. A beacon of something coaxed at me. I wished that feeling came more often, but it only seemed to manifest this easily when I searched for objects. It didn't seem to work for more complex matters involving humans. Maybe because I wasn't the most sociable? I never won the Popularity monthly contests the school hosted. Heck, I didn't even win the Funniest, the Most Beautiful, or the Smartest ones either. I was average it seemed. Maybe it was better that way. At least I wasn't bullied. I slid unnoticed through the petty dramas of high school.

Mr. Jackson's tell-tale jingling floated across my senses. I fist-bumped him instinctively, not truly seeing him until the sun hid behind a menacing thunderhead cloud. We'd have to hurry. He smiled at me, and I picked up the picnic basket.

The time it took for him to guide me on turning on the boat, undocking, scanning the lake to make sure we didn't collide with anyone else, took a good quarter of an hour. We settled in, and I tucked into the food vigorously, as he looked wistfully on.

"You sure the ring is here underwater, Cavilla?"

"I am pretty sure," I said around a mouthful of pastrami.

Mr. Jackson walked around the deck, flitting in and out of shadow as the sun played hide and seek above. After a while, he asked, "Have you been practicing?"

I flushed. "Some. I've been distracted with a lot of other things."

"Like that Poirot anthology you keep raving about?" he asked, chuckling.

"Yeah. And also helping friends at school with stuff…"

It would be too long to explain to him that in the past couple months I had found several peoples' misplaced Dick Tracy collections, found out the Cutest Couple of Pine Ridge High were in fact cheating on each other, and that the resident school clown kept urinating on the floor in his ongoing feud with the janitor. Never a dull moment.

Raising my head to see Mr. Jackson staring at me, I wondered if he didn't know already. Niko and Angelica made no secret of their spying on me when they came to visit. Surely, it must be part of whatever they did in their upstairs and downstairs visits. I wish I could ask Mr. Jackson about it, but he also didn't like to talk about it.

"Cavilla, make sure you keep practicing or you'll forget. You've got skills with that clarinet. Make sure your reeds don't dry out. Make sure you keep up with your sight reading. Are you going to perform in the local music fair?"

I wolfed down a hunk of Gouda cheese. "Maybe. I would love to, but I've heard the other kids. They're way better than me. And they perform cool klezmer stuff. All I know how to play is classical stuff. It's not popular. I don't think people will like that."

"You never know. People who go to those fairs come to hear different kinds of music. There is nothing wrong with classical music. But… Cavilla, if you want to try new genres, you can. Just because we stuck with classical doesn't mean you have to stick with it. Experiment! Try! I would have taught you other styles of music if it hadn't been for my death."

I nodded. He was right. But I was scared. Scared of trying new things, scared of standing out. I liked being overlooked by most people.

"You know, if you don't want to stay with music that is fine too. I think it would be a shame, but you've got to follow your dreams, your strengths. What do you want to do when you graduate?"

Three years until graduation. It seemed so far away. Yet, I'd fantasized so many times about life after high school.

"I want to be a private investigator. I want to take PI classes, after I take the aptitude test of course. Then I can get my Florida PI

Beginner's License. Once I get really good, I'll be able to have my own operation. I love helping people. Even if it gets icky sometimes, like if there's cheating, or murder, it's fun to find out stuff. As long as it helps people and doesn't hurt them."

Mr. Jackson smiled at me. "Are you able to take classes that can help you with that?"

"Not in high school, no. Other schools offer online classes in criminal psychology or forensics. But it's too hardcore for me. There *are* some PI classes online, but you have to be eighteen and above. It is recommended that private investigators know several languages. I'm going to try to take Spanish next year." Hopefully, it wouldn't be too difficult, as I heard it so often at home. It would certainly make Tia Luz Marina happy.

"It sounds like you're going to be busy. I'm so proud of you. Proud of what you're becoming. Keep it up. But don't forget to practice."

We laughed.

"Now about that ring…"

We spent the rest of the afternoon searching for it. I ended up diving in and scouting the lake bottom with my bare hands. Discouragement crept steadily in, with every unsuccessful dive. Mr. Jackson bravely persevered, helping me navigate the boat. I dove and skimmed the sand with my hands. I methodically mapped out every patch of area and dug like a dog each time. I watched for any glint of jewelry, any sparkle. My eyes were better than Mr. Jackson's. I didn't need glasses unlike him. I upturned rocks and weeds and other debris. I startled some fishes and eels.

My searching sped up as my determination increased. The dark storm clouds were rolling in menacingly. Pockets of lightning grumbled in them. I surfaced and resurfaced, gasping for air.

A flash of lightning illuminated the depths of the water, as I almost surfaced to end the search. A sparkle caught my eye. I dove in and dug at dark wooden rotted planks. The ring was caught on one of the ends. I grasped it and brought it up.

Mr. Jackson smiled, his being shimmering through the torrential rain. I gave it to him, the ring staying in my hand, yet duplicating as a ghost copy. That copy he took, and he thanked me. We hurried to take the boat back. I was in such a rush to get home, I didn't notice when he winked out of my plane of existence, peace steadying his essence. It wasn't until I stripped out of my sodden clothes that I realized we hadn't gotten to say goodbye. He wouldn't be back, of that I was sure.

***

It hurt that he was gone. But I was sure he had moved on, wherever 'on' was. To assuage my regret, I chattered at my Tia while she marinated a roast that night.

"Guess what, Tia? When I graduate, I'll be a PI! I'm even going to take Spanish to help. I'll get lots of Hispanic clients and be able to communicate."

Tia snorted. "About time for the Spanish. But hija, what is this about being a PI? That's a man's job. And it's not honorable. Better to be a secret agent or a criminal investigator. Those are real jobs. But still not jobs for a girl."

"That's sexist! Anyone can do it. I can do it. I help my friends all the time."

Tia slammed her whisk down. "The games you play with your friends is not real life, Cavillaca. I refuse to have my niece be a PI. Do something respectable like a scientist or lawyer."

I wrinkled my nose, my hands full of soy sauce. "It's not games. I've solved a lot of mysteries at school. I've helped a lot of people. And I want to keep doing it. Being a PI is respectable. The pay is all right. I'd be really good at it."

"Hija, you have to apply yourself. You need to leave your mystery books, your imagination behind. You've lived with me all your life, and you still don't know Spanish. You have average grades in school. You need to stand out. Apply yourself. Being a PI is foolish. No me hablas de eso mas. Basta."

My cheeks burned. In a fit, I slammed down the measuring cups and raced to my room. She didn't understand. She'd never understood. But I should have known. Trying to talk with Tia was like trying to pet an angry cat actively hissing and arching its back.

"Don't you dare slam the door!"

My hands shook but I gently closed the door and wept stormily afterward. I didn't often wish it, but sometimes, I wished I were raised by anybody else. Where were my parents? Other family? My uncle? No one told me anything, besides apply myself. Apply myself? Pah!

3

FAMILY MATTERS

A few days later

The lights refused to turn on. The major storm rolling over us had zapped our electricity hours ago. Ordinarily, I didn't mind the dark. But it made it hard to read. We were out of Virgen de Guadalupe candles. So, I tried to make bracelets by the tired gray light coming in through my bedroom window. But a niggling feeling made my skin crawl. My bathroom hallway beckoned insidiously with cold draughts and faint whispers. I turned to it, staring in the darkened space. Impalpable flashes of incongruous orange whisked over the darkness, a humming emerging from impossible corners, impossible depths. I pushed aside the beads and the strings, and got up, lured by the strange cinema happening. When I stepped into the hall, cold gripped at me, tenuous, pulling me forward. I screamed. The sensation stopped, and so did the bizarre humming. But just faintly in my perception, I heard fading murmurs. I jumped backward, resolving to get Tia's flashlight. I knew she had one somewhere. I didn't want to stay in my room any longer without light.

I sped through the house, and unashamedly went through Tia's drawers. She hid stuff in the unlikeliest places. As a kid I'd given up searching for items in their right place. But this was urgent. *Something* lived in my bathroom hallway. I'd sensed it for years. Sure, whatever it was only lived there part-time, but I didn't like it. Noise and light seemed to bother it. Well, I'd bother it right back.

I skimmed over her official documents, clothing, jewelry, and books. Still no sign of a flashlight. At a certain point, next to a melted Virgen Guadalupe candle, I saw some photos, and pieces of ripped up letters. My heart thudded. They were old photos. Black and white, the people dressed in 1930s or 40s clothing. Their faces were either blurred or scratched out, but I saw teases of dark hair on the people in the pictures.

I held up a swath of letters held together by a piece of twine. An odor of must and Tia's usual fragrance of overpowering jasmine and clay mingled together. Water stains adorned the top letter. The date read: El 5 de abril de 1934. I groaned. The entire rest of the letter was in Spanish. I caught a few words here and there, about travel, a boat, and home. Something about Peru, and home and animals. But the writing was hard to read, and I couldn't deal with the Spanish.

I sighed morosely. I had a great deal of work to do if I wanted Spanish-speaking clients once I had my PI business. I searched for more photos, but only found one that was clear and that had people in it. I skated past photos of earthen pots and villas in mountainsides. The photo that caught my eye was a huge gathering of people, nineteen adults next to each other, smiling and waving. They all had dark coloring and hair, and all the women looked alike. Some of the men's crazy mustaches or haircuts made it harder to see a family resemblance but there was one. They all resembled each other. Who was this huge family? And why did the women, their frizzy long dark hair, resemble mine so much? Some of their eyes, their lips, could have been duplicates of mine.

I sagged against the dresser, my heart skipping a beat. Were these people related to me? And Tia? I looked harder, yes, some of the women looked a lot like her.

I wondered if I should speak about this to Tia. We never spoke about family. A few years ago, I'd asked her about my parents, or her husband, and she had cut the conversation off in a fit of waving hands and sharply clanging bangles. The anger had radiated off her like a tea kettle coming to temperature.

But this… this needed some explanation. If only I knew *something*, anything about my origins. This might be a clue. I resolved to bring it up tonight when she came home from work. And I also made the decision to transcribe the letters and put them in a translator app. It was cheating, but I desperately wanted to understand the letters. I started to understand the notion of a language barrier more easily now. Truly a barrier, as effective as the Andean mountains, barring access to any but the most courageous.

I didn't want to go back to my bedroom. Things were much more interesting here. I sagged on Tia's bed and turned on the TV instead, quickly changing the channel from the wailing telenovela it was set on, to Cartoon Network.

***

That evening, Tia Luz Marina and I played poker. Or tried to. I was too easy to read. Then again, she'd only recently taught me how to play. We shuffled our cards in the gloom at our crappy cardboard table. We'd binged on popcorn and canned tuna, as she hadn't answered my call or read my texts about the power being out. We never had too much food in the house at any given time. Tia was the opposite of a hoarder.

I didn't mind an easy dinner. I munched on some popcorn contemplating my hand. But my thoughts kept straying to those letters and photos. Who were they? Where had they been going? Who had written to whom? The names had been blanked out. Who had taken such care to erase indicators? Tia? Or someone else?

Finally, I threw down my cards and adjusted the lantern Tia had managed to find in the garage.

"Tia, I have something to ask."

She sighed, her long hair trailing across the table and popcorn crumbs.

"Que ahora, hija?"

"I tried to find a flashlight today. I was in my room, and it was creepy and weird. I know there is something in the bathroom, I know it! So, I went looking for a flashlight, but finding anything in this house is complicated. I looked through your stuff–" Her eyes narrowed dangerously, but I pressed on. "I found a melted candle, very dangerous by the way I threw it out for you," I said babbling, "and found a packet of letters and photos. The letters are all in Spanish. And there are pics of tons of people I don't know. But they look like us. Who are they? Are they family? Are they in Peru? I understood something about Peru…"

I trailed off, and she closed her eyes breathing deeply. When she next opened them, she fixed me with a stare so full of complexity I couldn't decipher it before she launched in a quiet tirade.

"What were you doing going through my things? Have you no respect? Did I not teach you better than that? Looking for a flashlight? Pah. Good excuse."

I watched her closely, noting how artificial her voice sounded. She was manufacturing her anger, almost like she was stalling. Maybe my abysmal poker skills were rubbing off on her.

"Going through my things… I have private items in there, not for your eyes. I don't go through your stuff, do I? I would never invade your privacy like that."

"Tia," I said quietly. "What are those letters and pictures?"

She paused and her mouth wobbled.

"Cavillaca… They're memories of another time… They're old. Irrelevant. Besides, you can't read them because they're in Spanish."

"Tia, it's our family, isn't it?" I asked softly, more perplexed than angry at her attempts to distract.

She buried her face in her hands, her flan-colored skin like mine, flexing as she wrung them in her hair.

"Yes. Our early ancestors who came to America. I don't know all of them. I have only heard stories about them."

"We had a lot of ancestors then! That is so cool! But why are some of their faces scratched out in some pics?"

Tia Luz Marina stiffened. "It was necessary. Much power is contained in photographs. History is captured. Some of those people… It was safer to do it. Not all things are meant to be discovered, hija.”

"Power? You mean like magic?" I asked excitedly, pushing aside the bag of popcorn and cards. "What kind of magic? Are you into white or black magic?"

Tia snorted. "At least you know some measly part of our heritage. Unlike the Spanish–"

"Stop focusing on my not knowing Spanish! Or my heritage! It's not my fault you never want to talk about it. What are you so afraid of? What things aren't meant to be discovered? Family is family, and I have a right to know. You call me silly because I speak of ghost business in my bathroom hallway–"

"There are no ghosts in that bathroom, Cavillaca," she said and rolled her eyes.

"But you talk about power like magic is real. I hear you praying to the Incan gods of our past sometimes. I did some research, Tia. I know about Viracocha and Mama Quilla and–"

"Hush, hija! Don't say those names. Names, like photographs, have immense power. We don't want any untold eyes on us. Please don't force me to say anything more. I can't. I don't want anything to happen–" She broke down sobbing, crumpling on the table like a dying moth. I was still angry, still had too many questions bouncing around my head, but her tears chipped away at the anger. She hiccupped.

"I wish I could show you our home, our family tree. Tell you all the old stories. But I can't. You have to trust me. There is a good reason I can't."

"What if I don't trust you?" I said icily, more to get a reaction than because I actually meant it.

"Don't take that disrespectful tone with me," she warned, wiping away her tears. She regarded me, her large, dark eyes red and puffy. "I'm your protector, and I will tell you what you need to know. Be patient. Trust me."

"Trust goes both ways, Tia," I said, swiping at the poker cards and chips on the table. "You're hiding things from me. And I'll find out what it is, with or without your help. I'm going to be a PI, remember?"

I attempted to flounce out of the room, but theatrics had never been my game. As a parting shot, I shouted over my shoulder. "And there is something peculiar in my bathroom hallway! Ghosts or something else. I will never stop saying it."

For the first time in my life, I successfully slammed my bedroom door, and Tia didn't come down like a fury to berate me. Vaguely, I still heard her crying. It hit me then, the emotion I had seen in her eyes earlier. It hadn't been anger. It had been fear.

4

POINT OF NO RETURN

Dusk was seized by the fickle hand of fate, pausing in its steadfast itinerary into my bedroom. I let the light leech the color out of my room, immersing myself in the half-dread, half-excitement wake it brought. A sliver of sun still shone over the horizon, while a half moon glowed, frozen in the dust-colored sky. A pall of ochre covered its sullen face.

The light brought out Angelica and Niko's features better. This time, they lay on my bed, attempting to read some more of my Agatha Christie books. They leafed through *They Came to Baghdad*, *Evil Under the Sun*, *Death in the Clouds*, and *The Mysterious Affair at Styles*. I had a ton more, but that would keep them busy for a while. Niko had read most of those, but he'd forgotten a lot. Angelica, who'd read none of them, beamed like a toddler. They didn't mind that their ghostly forms shimmered through into reality. With concentration, they could push into this plane and make themselves corporeal. But it took effort.

I watched them, not engaging in their conversation this time. I felt melancholic and unfulfilled. I loved having my friends with me, but today, it just highlighted what I missed. The pets I'd had when I was a child. All dead now. Besides Niko and Angelica who were my best buds, I had no other real friends at school. The people I loved the most and had had great times with were all dead without exception. For the first time, I wished I were truly average, in the sense that I wished my life were completely normal.

As if in a perverse answer to my ponderings, the light streaming on my bed shimmered and thudded like a heartbeat. Coils of dust motes and sallow light danced together, forming the figure of a familiar animal. Matted white and gold fur, cloudy green eyes, a tail that flicked incessantly, and a purring that boomed in my bedroom like thunder. It couldn't be. It was Rumba, my beloved cat, my darling kitty who'd been with me since birth and who'd died that awful summer. She looked worn and tired, but she was here.

"Rumba? Is that really you?" I reached a hand, my fingers passing through her.

She meowed, jumping down on my star-shaped rug, and curling up next to me.

"Yes, dear Cavillaca," she said, rubbing her head against my hand.

Her voice was a low alto, underneath I almost sensed a masculine voice, deeper than hers, but then her voice went back to normal.

"You can talk?" I gaped. "Have you always been able to do that?"

She stomped on my legs and walked round in circles until she collapsed on my lap. Niko and Angelica whispered to themselves, pointing excitedly at her.

"You can talk..." I marveled, almost crying at the sight of her in my lap, weightless as a feather. I felt safe. I felt like a little girl again, like when she'd come and snuggle in bed with me during a storm. Or when I came home from school after being ignored by the teacher again, she'd greet me, purring and pawing at my ankles. Rumba was my rock. Unlike any human being in my life. Yes, even Tia. I glanced at the photo displays and collages on my bedroom dresser. Most of the photos were of Rumba and I; her as a kitten and me as a baby. Learning to ride a bike and her trotting next to me. My first day of kindergarten and her shedding her fur on my school uniform. On and on it went.

"I haven't always been able to talk," Rumba said in that queer double-edged voice. It almost sounded like Tuvan throat singing. "But after passing through, I met somebody. We joined as one and we travel between realms."

"Who did you merge with?" Niko asked, bounding from the bed and sitting next to me.

Rumba tottered for a bit as she went to him. Then, when she spoke, a deep voice resonated. "I am Ai-Apaec."

When I stared at him dumbly, he resumed loftily. "Mochican

god, creator of life, protector of the Moche."

"Why are you merged with my cat?" I asked dumbly.

"I am evolved from one of the ancient cat gods. It is an honor to serve you."

I raised my eyebrows. "If you're a god, shouldn't I be serving you?"

Niko and Angelica made shushing gestures as if I couldn't see them. They stared back sheepishly.

"I am a guide and guardian," Ai-Apaec said smoothly, modulating into Rumba's more dulcet tones.

"You mentioned realms. What realms?" I asked.

The deadened light flickered and whisked as a gale into my accursed bathroom hallway. The always ambient darkness pulsed and hummed. I shied away, ready to abandon everything. Irrationality flared through me. My friends and this god were out to kill me! The ghosts or monsters were going to get me! The humming intensified until it reverberated in my bones, making my entrails and teeth chatter. A whiff of salt, like ocean brine, reached me. The darkness frittered away, bit by bit, until a copper-tinged tunnel revealed itself to us, gleaming wickedly. Steam or smoke billowed out, caressing our faces with the tantalizing invitation to enter. Rumba/Ai-Apaec walked to the entrance and sat regally next to it, eyeing me with cool green eyes.

"Enter and meet your destiny."

I shrank away, shaking my head. Goosebumps erupted on my flesh. A sickening feeling rose in my stomach. That presence I'd felt for so long was not as sharp and menacing. But roiling echoes of spookiness reached me, poking me. There was dead out there.

Rumba continued to wait, and so did my friends. They wouldn't lead me to danger. Would they? Swallowing, I stumbled forward, stopping just before the entrance. Sweat rolled off my forehead, dropping on my flowered blouse, and into my long, dark hair.

"There are ghosts in there," I whispered. "I'm afraid."

Rumba looked at me peaceably. "You? You're never afraid of anything. You're a curious human, always checking out things. Don't tell me you're afraid now? And of ghosts much less? You talk with them all the time. As a child of Supay, you should embrace your heritage–"

Angelica and Niko exploded in a fit of coughing. They threw themselves dramatically on the floor and rolled around. I stared at them bemusedly, wishing I could throw something at them.

"Are you done?" I asked acidly when they stopped.

Rumba shifted uneasily.

"What heritage? What's Supay? What's beyond that tunnel? There are more ghosts aren't there? I feel them all the time. But I'm scared." I rubbed my arms nervously. "There's danger. I feel that too. Is it just my imagination?"

Rumba shifted as if to come to me, to rub her body on mine like she used to. But she stayed where she was, still managing to look regal. "You have to find out for yourself. Come Cavilla."

I hesitated, reeling from the smell of copper and sea salt. Once I entered, there was no going back. I knew that as certainly as I knew time would have to resume at some point. What was the worst that could happen? I'd meet more ghosts? I'd finally find out what upstairs and downstairs were? I glanced at Niko and Angelica, looking the most serious as I'd ever seen them. They flanked me, each attempting to put a hand on my shoulder.

With Rumba, with my friends, I could do anything. Anything beat being here, straddling two worlds, being average, being reprimanded by Tia, being in the dark about too many aspects of my life. Taking a deep breath, I stepped into the tunnel.

****

A muted cold gripped at me, in swirling clouds of steam, or fog. I waved it away, focusing on the road forward, one step at a time. I squinted my eyes, focusing on that intangible feel as I did back in my bedroom; like the world was tilted, reality slightly off-kilter. I walked faster, the humming reducing in volume into almost an enjoyable purr. Rumba walked beside me, her tail curled up high. Niko and Angelina trailed me like bodyguards, foregoing their usual chatter.

Eventually, the fog lifted, and the dark cocoon tinged with copper and fear erased itself from around us. I stepped foot on a deck, and almost lurched forward. A foghorn blasted, and I jumped. Niko and Angelica dashed forward, zooming to one end of the large steamship we found ourselves aboard. For a moment, I jumped out of my own body, and I saw a panoramic view of the boat, its mighty girth breaking through the ocean waves, frothy laments splashing vigorously on a white hull. Some of the foam splashed so high, it reached the cabins near the top of the ship. In the next moment, I was back in my body, fighting nausea. Rumba snuck close to me, purring. I pet her mechanically, willing the nausea down, trying to discern the strange happenings on the ship. There were some people, but not a lot. All were dressed in modern clothing, but they all ignored each other. One person read the newspaper, one was on his phone, another played video games, one read a book. Some were staring overboard at the horizon, immobile, fixated on something I couldn't see. Angelica and Niko poked at some of them, but the other ghosts shook them off gently and moved aside. Angelica and Niko seemed more real here, less gauzy. So did Rumba. I tried looking at the horizon, but nothing but sea surrounded us.

"What is this place?" I asked Rumba. More waves unfurled around the boat, smacking it heartily. The foam landed on my face, and I licked the saltiness away.

"It is a docking bay of sorts between the living and the dead," Rumba explained, licking her paw studiously.

"So, a purgatory?"

"Not quite. Although most souls here you will find need some help. It depends on what you focus on here. The dead can go in any realm they choose technically."

"How many realms are there? What is this, if it's not really purgatory?"

"You know nothing, do you?" Rumba said plaintively. "You need to look up your heritage and the myths. There you will find your answers."

Tia had refused to teach me about my Peruvian, my proud Incan heritage. It seemed I had to take matters into my own hands. Surely, any culture had some version of heaven, hell, and purgatory. Whatever this place was, it was a close equivalent to purgatory. But what did these souls need?

I approached a tall older man smoking a cigarette. He turned to face me, and a blast of essence wracked me: sensations of despair, cigarette-infested apartments, surfing at the beach, a little girl running to a playground, a little coffin being lowered in the ground, his own lowered next to a mound of fresh earth. She'd been murdered, and so had he shortly after. He'd been looking for her murderers. His gaze locked into mine, and he extended his tanned hands.

"Please help me."

I wheezed and stepped back a few paces. He disengaged, and those sensations released me. He had the same basic essence as that of Niko, Angelica, or Mr. Jackson. An urgency within his soul, an agitation that called for soothing. But his levels were beyond what I'd ever felt. His anguish clawed at my guts. If he needed help, he needed it asap. The only problem was I wasn't sure I could help. Helping friends was one thing. This was another. And why, why was it me? Because I liked to sleuth? Tons of other high schoolers loved that stuff, and nothing magical happened to them. What made me so special?

I toured the deck sensing, thankfully, small urgencies from other dead; snippets of small missions—finding a precious relic, wanting information on a deceased family member, vexations of legal clauses that muddled wills. I stayed away from the few dead who radiated a sharper sense of urgency. As I circulated around the deck, a staircase appeared. I took it, and landed on another deck, despite my original view of the ship not matching with this. A few more dead revealed themselves to me, this time dressed in early twentieth century garb. How large was this ship? How many decks did it have? As soon as the thought struck me, another staircase appeared. I went down that one, and nineteenth century ghosts ambled around, stuck in their own reveries. I went down a few more levels before becoming overwhelmed. All the ghosts tugged at me with varying levels of urgency. Every so often, I fell on a dead person who seemed utterly relaxed, no urgency pulling at me.

When I climbed the staircases up toward the main deck, some of those relaxed dead followed, but didn't speak to me. I got sensations of memories, but nothing more. A Victorian lady and a Chinese wood maker flew up the staircase and vanished.

A working theory bubbled in my mind. Some of these dead didn't need help. They were here to chill. They seemed to have more mobility between decks, between times. Those who had urgency were locked to the deck they were on. I observed a few more ghosts as I climbed the last few levels. Yup, those who had unfinished business moved around, but made no effort to go out, and they didn't vanish from view like the others.

I climbed the last staircase with my own sense of urgency. So many called to my senses. Their needs were like infinite bubbles stewing inside my brain. I couldn't help them all, certainly not today, all at once.

I pondered again. What made me so special? Rumba had mentioned something earlier. Child of Supay. What did it mean? As I thought it, a howling wind ruffled across me. Thunder rolled and a pale white light spidered through the clouds. My skin prickled.

"It is time to go," Rumba said, materializing in front of me. "I will take you back. Eventually, you'll be able to come along on your own. Follow me. Hurry, child."

I followed, straining to see Angelica and Niko. They were on the deck, tussling with each other over a sack of marbles. Hey! Those were my marbles. But while they waved goodbye at me, worry strained their faces. Rumba looped back and butted me in the ankles.

"Hurry," she said calmly, and I followed, wondering why despite her calm, the fur on her back stood on end.

5

GUMSHOE

Life resumed normally, my days spent rifling through school library books, looking for any hints, any familiar names in the mythology sections. The few books I found on Incan mythology were thin and devoid of useful information. Some were quite old, out of date, and when I showed them to my Latino friends, they laughed and said none of the material was authentic; it was all from the conquistadors' point of view and ensuing Catholicism, effectively twisting our mythology into something it wasn't. I just wished I'd known about all this sooner, or that I could ask Tia. But ever since our discussion that night, I felt a strain between us, a strain best left unattended, through trivial conversations and sideways glances.

Between moments of normalcy, of attempting to use the school internet to do research (which mostly ended in disconnection and a flurry of maddening beeps), of Tia offhandedly mentioning my quinceañera next year, and reading more Agatha Christie novels, were those moments where time stopped, and I stepped into that portal in my bathroom to that in-between platform I couldn't name. Those moments on the ship, with Rumba as my guide, observing the dead and getting a handle on the atmosphere layered themselves into my life like an overstuffed mil hojas dessert.

Eventually, I managed to find books in the public library that talked about the old gods of Incan lore. There weren't that many, especially compared to the bloated Greek or Norse mythologies, where gods abounded. I learned more about Pacha Mama, Viracocha, Illapa, and Supay. The latter I couldn't pronounce. I'd done research a while ago, but it had been brief and superficial. Now I had access to more sources. I looked up more about the legends and the worlds that lay in the cosmos: hanan pacha, kay pacha and ukhu pacha. The "real" world was kay pacha. But I'd discovered yet another world, that wasn't mentioned in any of the books. Surely it had to have a name? In my head, I called it the In-Between. I burned to ask Tia or Rumba how to pronounce the names, but I ignored the former, and Rumba kept mum about gods after that first foray into the In-Between.

One evening, as I went back to the In-Between, this time without Angelica and Niko, I fell on the very first dead I'd met when I'd first come—that tall, lonely gentleman whose urgency had left me dizzy. He regarded me with guarded eyes, and Rumba looked solidly on, silently encouraging.

I held out a hand, part wave, part beseeching.

"Tell me more," I asked simply.

"My little girl," he replied, a tremor in his voice. "I only saw her on the weekends. My ex-wife and I were in the middle of a long, nasty divorce. Lauren was a bright child. Goofy, loud, crazy. She played outside all the time."

He fell silent and contemplated the crashing waves overboard.

"Then, she started to become quiet. Didn't want to talk to me. She hated going outside. I tried to talk to her, and my ex. No one could tell me what was going on. I did what I could; I put kiddy movies on and games to keep Lauren busy. But that little girl wasn't right."

He hesitated and tottered a bit.

"I got a call from the police one morning… They'd found two bodies in the woods. My girl and my ex. Beaten to death. The car was at her house, the keys in her purse. All they had was their clothing. The police thought I was responsible; I was the last one who had seen them alive. I knew my wife saw other men. But the police didn't have records of them. I got belligerent. I stayed in jail for a bit. They didn't have enough evidence to keep me. I constantly kept looking for news of the killer. But nothing. When the case finally turned cold, I hunted for that son of a gun high and low. I knew it was a man; women don't commit atrocities like that. I went through the address book I had memorized of hers and hunted for every man she'd been in contact with. Learned squat. Then, one night, I wake up to smoke a cig, and somebody stuffs a pillow over my face, in my own bed."

"You think it's the same person that killed your ex-wife and daughter?" I asked, seeing the conviction in his eyes.

"Yes. But I don't know who it is," he murmured.

"How do you think I can help?" I asked, crossing my arms. Sleuthing in the real world, or kay pacha I could do. How the heck would I pull it off in this place?

"You can. You are here," he said as truthfully as a child.

I reigned in my frustration. People here knew something I didn't. That was a mystery that needed to be solved yesterday. The mystery of my identity. My powers. But this man's anguish was more urgent. If I was here, and he was here, there was a reason. It was clear I had a job to do. Would it be this difficult once I became a PI? Is this what adults did at their jobs? Just wing it? I truly hoped not.

Yet, wing it I would, as I had no idea what I was supposed to do. Look for clues. But I would need to go to the crime scene. Have some visual at least.

"What do I do?" I mouthed at Rumba.

Rumba shook her head, silently urging me to trust myself.

I huffed.

I touched the man, Reggie, but no images or essence grabbed at me. A maddening flurry of jumbled feelings and thoughts came through in a vortex though, like a swarm of bees zipping crazily past. He was too agitated. Or was it me? I trembled a fair bit myself.

I looked overboard, and across the deck. Nothing. I eyeballed the water, thinking about whether to jump in. But knowing how the world worked with my luck, I'd drown and lose my soul or something. Instead, I decided to go into the heart of the steamship. I barged through the oak doors, stalked past the bar and the mess hall, arriving at the top of the polished stairwell. There were no dead there. Rumba followed me, purring, a bell jingling on her collar.

"Am I going the right way?" I asked.

She stared sardonically back, wordlessly.

"Fine. I'll figure it out."

I climbed down, down, down, for what seemed an eternity. Every so often I heard a sharp regular metallic clang, like someone was mining or doing metallurgy. I descended through eerie, dark halls until finally I reached a floor with two doors. The white doors were small, like doors to a locker. Big black lock wheels set in the middle intimidated me. I listened hard for that metallic sound, but it was gone. Flicking my hair back, I opened the first door to my left, slowing turning the lock wheel. A whiff of humidity hit my nose, and I edged the door open. I peeked in, not daring to actually enter. A night sky flowered around me in a breath of stars highlighting a wide full moon. Fields of sunflowers and weeds rippled beyond dusky valleys. A cave entrance dripping with water materialized in front of me, majestic, imposing. Its cold surface gleamed, and I reached out ready to touch that damp, chilled marbled rock. It stretched upward, as if there was a trail ascending into the heavens. A calm wind rustled through my hair, bringing with it odors of swamp and sun tan lotion, sounds of cicadas and swishing of palm tree fronds, like home. Vertigo assailed me, the stars and moon chasing each other across the sky, the cave whirling in my senses.

Backing away, I retreated until the door closed, and I stood on the deck shivering.

"What… what was that place?" I asked Rumba who sat imperiously next to the banister.

"Remember your readings," she replied.

Sighing, I waited for the shivering to pass, then I ogled the other door and twisted it open. A blast of heat surged out stinging my eyes. The fetid stench of moldy water made me gag, and I stepped into a red haze of steam. It almost looked like the tunnel entrance leading to the In-Between, but the sound of dripping water was incessant, and the heat made me sweat. A low rumble pulsed like a bellows being worked. I ventured out slowly, careful not to step in the rancid streams at my feet. A cave tunnel opened, boring itself into the ground. I looked up, searching for a sky. There was none. The bellows' sound mounted to a steady shriek in the background. A heat wave blasted from the tunnel, and a thudding, like gigantic footsteps, reverberated everywhere.

"Get out," came Rumba's echoing voice, magnified ten times. "You're not ready yet. Get out!"

I looked behind me, to see the door's opening shrinking, becoming farther away. I leaped by sheer instinct and jumped across the water to land through the door, banging my right side as I rolled and landed mostly on the deck. My legs were still dangling. Heaving, I hoisted myself up and tucked my legs in just as the door swung shut with a metallic clang.

Flopping on the deck, I lay on my back, letting the lulling of the ship calm my frantically beating heart. Rumba curled up next to me, and I stroked her, her warmth stilling my fear.

"Be careful when you go through that door," Rumba said after a few minutes.

"Why would I ever want to go through *that* door again?" I said incredulously.

"Remember your readings and research."

"You keep saying that," I said, propping myself up on one elbow. "Is this about the gods? The myths?"

I trailed off. Two doors. One with serenity feels, and the other with creepy feels. Heaven and hell? No. That was the bastardized version of what the conquistadors had done to our culture.

"Hanan pacha and uku pacha?" I whispered.

Rumba's sudden purring was as good as an affirmation.

"I can access them through these doors," I said in awe.

But how would that help Reggie? And others like him? Heck even Angelica and Niko? I flopped down again in consternation. Upstairs and downstairs. This was what they had talked about. The dead with unfinished business could travel from realm to realm. Apparently, I could too. But I had to be careful, especially with uku pacha.

I felt so lost. I had all this awesomeness and didn't know what to do with it. A niggling thought kept pushing at me. In the books

I'd read, the power of nature and water was sacred. Water especially was a connecting source between realms. So, water was the answer? We were surrounded by water. We were on a ship. Maybe I just needed to dive in and swim…

"You cannot go in the water," Rumba said. "You will lose your hold to the realms and be forever lost."

Crap. There had to be another way then.

"Why me?" I asked plaintively.

Rumba didn't answer.

***

I threw myself headlong into more research. I stopped looking at English sources. They were sparse. Perhaps I'd have more luck with Spanish sources. Unfortunately, that meant learning Spanish. I started spending time with the Spanish club after school, observing in the back even though I wasn't officially part of the club. Conjugations, conversations, sentence stems all bored into my brain. Sometimes I cheated and used the dictionary to translate word by word what I found in reference texts. It was hard and long, and by the end of the day my hand cramped terribly.

In the meantime, I visited Niko and Angelica's death site. But I found nothing new. Like with Reggie, I'd have to find answers in the In-Between. Through my bloated brain fog from school, Spanish, and mythology reading, a key word stood out in my research: water. Any source of water was a connecting point to access different realms. Logically, the only option for me, was to access the water points through the two boiler rooms I'd gone through the entrances to hanan and uku pacha. How exactly that would help me with the dead I wasn't sure. To be able to solve some of these crimes, or even the milder cases of theft or misplaced items, I'd need to be able to go where the dead used to live. I'd been able to do it for Niko, Angelica, and Mr. Jackson because they were local. But how could I help Reggie, who'd lived in Minnesota?

I'd figure it out, like I did with everything else. It would just take time. I didn't have a ticking clock after all.

I actually learned more when I wasn't actively searching. One day, during my tryst to the In-Between, I chilled next to the spirit of a young businessman. He kept checking his briefcase and staring at his watch. No urgency radiated from him. He was here for pleasure mostly, though I was sure he normally would be found somewhere in hanan pacha. After watching him repeat the pantomime for a bit, I kicked at a water puddle causing the shivering as droplets to land on my face. It rippled, and so did he. I kicked at the puddle again and the spirit dropped in the puddle, his jacket lapels swishing as he sank in. Not to be beaten, I splashed straight into the puddle and found myself sinking slowly, the wetness wrapping around me and sloughing off.

Time seemed to stretch and drip steadily, like molasses of the cosmos filtering down. I came out into a sunny, arid day, next to a train station. The gentleman, Arnold, I believe, though he'd never talked to me, walked from the sidewalk to the tracks, the decrepit orange buildings looming over him, their blackened windows peering down indifferently. People walked their dogs, jogged, hurried to work. Somehow, they seemed less real than Arnold. The cityscape itself appeared as an illusory daydream, wavering like a drop of watercolor paint about to fall. There was no urgency there, no danger. I could sit and stare at the stores and the glittering sun as it chased its happiness between the clouds.

Spending time there, in someone else's world, was the calmest thing I'd done in a while. No need to investigate. No need to learn, no need to translate. Just be and observe. I knew it was temporary. Real life, the kay pacha, would call my attention sooner rather than later. As well as my otherworldly responsibilities if I ever found what they were and how to do them.

Arnold sat on the bench by the station and flipped through the documents in his briefcase. People came and went, checking schedules, wandering about, waiting for the train. A woman came and sat on the bench, reading a book. Her long, blonde hair swept over her heart-shaped face as she read quickly, fingers and pages flipping fast. Arnold stared at her, a smile on his face.

"She comes every day," he said wistfully, his gravelly voice a shock.

"Does she?" I asked, recovering from the surprise of hearing him speak to me finally.

"Yes. In a few minutes she will feed the pigeons."

Sure enough, after a while she closed her book and dug into her bag for dried bread. He observed her intently, not jumping as the train whistle pierced the air. The woman gathered her things and mounted the train along with the other passengers.

As the train departed, I asked Arnold, "Did you know each other?"

"No."

After a pause, he added, "We never even spoke to each other. But I enjoyed watching her, and her books."

I nodded. I stayed there with him on the bench, watching trains come and go. Then, the landscape trembled, and it was late morning again, the sun high in the sky, and the routine repeated. Arnold came and sat on the bench, and she eventually came, reading a book and feeding the pigeons. After a few reiterations of this, I realized that we were stuck in a loop. A memory? His favorite memory perhaps?

The landscape shuddered again, but this time the train was late. The woman sighed and called someone, though her words were lost to the intangibility of the world around us.

"Is this a memory?"

"No," Arnold said. "This is the recent past. I was already dead. I haven't experienced this."

"Oh."

We sat there, and the day went by. People stuck in their daily routines, the passing of time advancing normally, until sunset appeared, punching through with bright, striated colors. Arnold fidgeted next to me, opening his mouth a few times, but not saying anything. What was this place? A memory, or the recent past? How did the transition happen? Did it happen for every dead? Were we in the In-Between, the pachas or some blend of everything? What were the rules here?

All at once, the two scenes overlaid each other: that sunlit morning with the arrival of the train, and the woman in a loop, then the normal passing of time at a different speed with Arnold's memory playing normally in front of my eyes, and the other scene advancing at a snail's pace, infinitesimally slow.

"Does this usually happen?" I asked, my brain hurting from the schism in reality.

"No. I think you're causing this," he said, looking around

cautiously.

"How?" I breathed.

"You're overthinking things," he laughed. "You are strong. You're seeing into multiple dimensions at the same time."

I stared dumbly. How?

I phrased it out loud, but he didn't respond. The scene shivered again and my head split.

"I need to go back," I said, "This is a lot to handle."

"Sure." He held out an arm, and I took it.

We walked away from the station and headed toward the puddle we'd fallen through. Up we went, sucked in toward the sky, and we were spat out on the steamship's deck in the In-between.

Arnold floated away toward the main cabin, headed to the staircase leading to the two doors, I was sure. I sat on the deck, panting a little, my head pounding.

Angelica and Niko ran to me, abandoning their checkers game.

"You're back! How did it go?" they asked.

"Confusing," I mumbled.

"Come with us," Angelica said, tugging at my arm. "Hang out with us," she nodded at the puddle I'd used with Arnold. "You'll get more answers to your questions. It won't be as confusing."

"Guys, I'll take a rain check on that," I said, squeezing my temples. "It's been a long day. Later, okay?"

Barely holding in their frustration, they went back to their game. Rumba sauntered out of the cabin, and ran to me, butting her head against my legs.

"Time to go back?" she asked.

"Yes."

***

To forget the reality-twisting events of the In-Between, I distracted myself by going into Tia's bedroom and finding the letters and pictures. She'd put them back in the same hiding spot in the drawer. I was surprised she hadn't hidden them somewhere else or gotten rid of them. Maybe she did want me to learn more about our family after all.

I quickly read through the letters but didn't understand much more than the first time around. My Spanish was improving, but not that quickly, darn it!

It seemed a manual translation was in order. I'd have to transcribe the letters and translate word for word using a dictionary. But that was so tedious and boring. Instead, I skimmed through, and noted down all the proper names I could find in my Mysteries of Life notebook: Manuela, Jose, Eduardo, Gloria, Pablo, Camilla, Dolores. At one point I saw Tia Luz Marina's name and another woman's: Celestina. I rifled through the pictures, seeing if there were dates or names, but no luck. That one clear picture I had found with the nineteen people in it smiling and laughing, really looked like a relic of the 1940s. I found a few more with the faces scratched out, but I focused on the clothing this time: two children holding hands, seemed to date from the late 50s or 60s. Just to make sure, I compared with the photos in the heavy tome we had in our library: *Historical Encyclopedia of Costumes*. My estimate was correct. Spurred by a sudden desire to find other clues, I unabashedly searched through the rest of Tia's bedroom. I found my birth certificate and Tia's. I scribbled the information in my notebook and put everything back in its place.

I read one more time through the letters and noticed a few proper names I'd missed: Ollantaytambo and Chinchero. Surely, they were names of places, not people.

Struck by a brainwave, I searched through Tia's closet, hunting for her Peruvian passport. I flipped through and found multiple entry and departure dates from Peru to New Jersey, Peru to Wisconsin, Peru to Colorado, and Peru to Florida. I dropped the passport back, stunned. I didn't know she'd traveled so extensively in the United States. The entry date to Florida, the place I'd been all my life, was stamped as February 19th, 1986. Three years after my birth. I scoured my memory, trying to recall my life before the US. But all I got was a vague feeling of unease, urgency, almost akin to the sensation I'd felt from the bathroom hallway before I'd discovered the In-Between. Or that presence I'd felt when I'd opened that second door to uku pacha. I looked through more entry dates. In the 50s and 60s were a lot of trips to Europe – France, England, Poland,

Italy, and Hungary.

Well, it was set. I would have to do research and see if the US Census had records of my family. I could start cross referencing the names I'd written down with our last name, Ramirez, though I knew it would be difficult. Ramirez was a popular last name after all. Immigration records and visa information might be found there too. I'd have to figure out how to contact them, who to contact.

I would do as much as I could by myself. I was a big girl after all. I wanted to see how much I could achieve on my own. But sooner or later I'd need Tia's help. And when the time came, I would push her to tell me everything. If the dead couldn't help with my other problems and give me answers, I would make sure she would. There were too many secrets to unravel.

6

FAMILY ROOTS

Water. The key to the In-Between and the realms was water. I went in after my incursion with Arnold and couldn't do anything because there was no water available. Improvising, I dashed out to kay pacha, despite Rumba's protests that she couldn't keep up, sped through my bedroom, into the kitchen and took out one of Tia's washing basins from under the sink. Reeling from the residual smell of old Fabuloso clinging to the basin, I filled it to the top with water. Aiming for the perfect stride to not spill water, but hurry back to the In-Between, I lugged the basin all the way to the deck. I splashed all of it upon the deck and called one of the "relaxed dead" as I called them (easier to say than un-urgency feeling dead)— the spirit of a little boy. Together, we plunged into his memory of roller skating with his friends after baseball practice. If I kept my mind blank, I could enjoy the memory with him, and nothing strange happened. The clacking of their wheels on the asphalt numbed my brain into compliance. If I thought too hard about the other dimensions, about other points in time, the memory started to fritter apart.

So, I practiced staying in the now, focusing on someone other than myself.

Eventually, I got the hang of it, and when I did, I resurfaced on the steamship deck. I smiled excitedly. Soon, I'd be ready for Angelica and Niko, and memory hopping with them.

I cringed a little as Reggie stepped onto the deck, his mournful eyes, catching mine. I hadn't forgotten him. But his speechless gaze by itself was a reproach. If I could get my powers under control, I knew I could help him.

I breathed out. One thing at a time.

***

After I dumped a basin of water on the deck, I jumped in after Niko and Angelica. I relished the in-stasis feeling gently tugging at me, then squealed as I popped out smack onto the pier outside Mr. Jackson's house. Angelica and Niko were taking off the chains of their bikes, glancing up at their home, the two-story coral house right next to Mr. Jackson's eggshell white humbler abode. The garden was lushly alive, rows of gardenias and begonias proudly thrusting up past well-manicured hedges.

This was a memory then. This was before their death, before their mom lost herself in her grief and let everything die.

My friends waved at me, and I peeked at my own bike, chained up next to theirs. We had so many memories together that started here. But which specific memory did they choose, and why? I realized the dead showed nothing random.

I jumped on my bike and followed them, the late afternoon sun beating on our backs. They almost seemed completely real, their shirts flapping in the wind. We whizzed past speed bumps, whacked past tufts of Spanish moss, and at each pier we passed, one shouted "Gator!" or "No Gator!" I smiled, carefully watching the stick-like figures that bobbed on the lake water, or the cypress shoots that stood out impassively when there were no gators. Every so often, Angelica yelled "Duck!" and we had to guess if it meant ducking from the massive oak trees we cycled under, or if there was a family of ducks nestled in the shoots. Sadly, we saw no ducks.

We whizzed on by and caught up to an ice cream truck slowly making its rounds. Its bright, corny music lured us in, and just like we had that day, Angelica ordered chocolate, Niko strawberry, and I pistachio.

We settled on a bench with our ice cream, in the mini park the city had built a couple decades before. Somewhere in the distance, whining lawnmowers revved to life, the soundtrack to our lazy Saturdays. My ears hummed as the conversation we'd had back then started up. We'd chattered on and on about the latest assignments, the new book club, the increasing ice cream flavors, the demolition of the lake gazebo, and our latest reads. True to form, I'd been reading an Agatha Christine, a Marple mystery for a change, and my friends had both started *Sabriel* by Nix. I distanced myself from the memory mentally, focusing instead on the birds in the trees, the far-off cries of kids screaming in play, the dim roar of motorboats on the lake.

With a sigh, I recalled more memories with them: dashing through neighbors' backyards playing hide and seek; hopping around in the shores of the lake, trying to startle fish; races from the piers to our homes at sunset; climbing trees and trying to recite passages from our favorite books while upside down. I didn't even remember how we met– that's how long ago our friendship began.

I should have been grateful; they'd come back even after death, and we created new memories. Being here now in the In-Between was a once in a lifetime opportunity to relive their best memories. And yet… yet, I recognized it as a frail simulacra. It couldn't last forever. I enjoyed my time with them like a miser, I clung to our precious moments together when they came to see me, or me them. But they wouldn't be here forever. Sooner or later, I'd solve the mystery of their death, and they would leave me for good, like Mr. Jackson had. I wasn't sure I could bear it.

Was I cocky for assuming I could solve their death after a simply classified closed case hit and run? Perhaps. But I'd done more impossible things. It was my duty to help them. There was a way to solve it, I was sure of it. However, it also meant letting them go.

My mind wandered to the boiler rooms. I hadn't gone back since my first visit. Perhaps I'd be able to visit them afterwards in the hanan pacha. If I could find them. A realm of the upper gods, surely it wouldn't be easy to find whoever I wanted. An infinite realm with infinite dead wasn't as easy as navigating our small suburban neighborhood. I forced myself back to the present, tuning back in to the conversation. Angelica and Niko had taken out blank cards and drew anime illustrations for everyone in our class. That was back in fifth grade. It was supposed to have been a prank on our classmates: everyone got a card, but everyone got a level and type of card. The kind ones in the class got Hero cards, the regular ones in the class got cards based on what we knew of their interests and hobbies, and the mean ones in the class got images of supervillains and butts. I was supposed to come up with tag lines for each category of card.

I smiled, remembering that our prank had almost gotten us in trouble with the teacher at first. Thankfully, no one knew Niko and Angelica drew anime. And I'd created generic enough lines that no one suspected me. But it had been fun seeing the laughs on everyone's face, and the frowns and grumbling from the mean kids. We'd been smart enough to leave no evidence behind, and in the end, the teacher had determined it wasn't malicious enough to warrant serious questioning or pursuit.

I wanted to hang onto that goofy memory. But my mind kept spinning back around to my friends' death. A simple hit and run at 8:45pm at night, December 12, 1995. They'd been taking out the garbage. The police came. What their photos showed were the strewn garbage bins and litter everywhere in the garden; the skidding tire tracks, nicked mailboxes and garden ornaments from surrounding neighbors. According to the police reports, interviews had led to nothing: no one had seen anything. A bit of blue car paint had been found on the bins, and one mailbox, but that was it. Someone had heard a high pitched squeal, but they hadn't made it to the window in time to see anyone. I'd managed to infer, based on the photos, the reports, and the injuries my friends had described, that a mid-size vehicle had hit them, a vehicle with grill overlay, due to grill marks on one mailbox. I'd analyzed the pictures of the tire tracks and had called on one of my Tia's friends, who worked with cars, to help me identify which tires had a similar or identical tread, and which cars had a similar paint as the one discovered at the scene. He'd narrowed it down to Ford Bronco, Land Rover, or Jeep Wrangler. But we hadn't gotten beyond that.

I wondered if I could have Niko and Angelica relive that memory; though they'd repeated countless times they'd heard the car, but not fast enough to jump out of the way before it crushed them. They'd confirmed it had been a blue vehicle, but nothing more. It had been too dark to notice anything more. A thunderstorm had zapped the public lighting a few days before.

A thought occurred to me. Maybe some neighbors had had security footage of their homes at the time. We didn't have any traffic lights, except for the main road, which had no red light cameras. Speaking of cameras, I recalled that a couple of our neighbors had dash cams because they had extra fancy cars, and they were constantly worried they'd be stolen. Surely the police would have asked them for footage? But I knew the sheriff in charge of the case had been close to retirement, and his last few cases had sputtered into rapidly closed cases. I wasn't even sure if his team had interviewed the neighbors. Why hadn't I thought of that before? I could do it.

Perhaps it might be easier to ask my friends to relive the memory of that night. It was a traumatizing thing to ask, and I was hesitant to interrupt our idyllic foray in the past. But it would help. The scene around us shivered, and my friends stared at me wide-eyed, their forms duplicating and overlapping themselves. Their new forms shook their hands vehemently.

"Please don't. We can't remember anything anyway."

"Cavilla, if it were so easy, we would have told you."

Sighing, I released my grip on their memory, and the afternoon relaxed back into normalcy. The idle chatter we'd been engaged in resumed, and I attempted to let go of my frustrations. All in due time, I would get answers. Nothing in life was easy. Even supernatural stuff it seemed; perhaps especially the supernatural wasn't easy.

We enjoyed the rest of the memory of that afternoon, playing tag, scaling up the trees, tossing Spanish moss at each other, drawing makeshift Cluedo rooms in the dirt and pretending we were Mr. Green or Mrs. Peacock.

In the end, we decided to bicycle back to our starting point instead of just honing on a wet spot. The shadows of the late afternoon flicked over me, like playful bats flitting repeatedly over our heads. Angelica and Niko bicycled in front of me, yelling "Duck!" I nonchalantly glanced at our neighbors' houses, noticing how some had changed paint color, or some hadn't built a pool yet, or had fewer cars than now. As I continued to scan my attention every which way, a part of my brain registered the back of a blue car at Mrs. Peloza's house, parked next to a gray sedan, and the back of a blue SUV at the old couple's house– the Capidaglis. I stored the information away in the back of my mind.

When I went back to my world, the kay pacha, I would ask those neighbors about their car, and what they'd heard the night of the hit and run. It wouldn't hurt to ask. With enough luck, I would get more leads on the preliminary searching I had done and finally find Angelica and Niko's killer.

***

I had to put my sleuthing to the side for a few weeks as our school prepared itself for the Halloween concert: a classical repertoire first from composers like Grieg or Mussorgsky, and then a contemporary finish with modern music. Some of the classical pieces had been arranged for clarinet. Sadly, one of the star clarinet players broke her arm two weeks before the concert and no one was interested in replacing her. In addition, one of the pieces needed a clarinet quartet. Michele, who did choir, begged me to intervene and help them out. The band teacher swooped on me after lunch one day and asked me to help. I had no choice but to obey. A secret part of me also relished practicing for a modern repertoire, even if it had been too long since I'd last practiced. But I refused to let panic set in.

As soon as I came home from school, I practiced. After dinner, I practiced. Tia raised an eyebrow but said nothing of my new habits.

The day before the concert, I drafted a paper form to The National Archives and Records Administration, requesting visa information and immigration documents. I just needed names. I really needed to talk to Tia. But now was not the time.

***

After the success of the Halloween concert, I was forcibly dragged into participating in band. Even though the deadline for registering had passed, the instructor insisted I be let in, as other students had dropped out. I could almost feel Mr. Jackson's smile, through the realms.

I forced myself to target my energy on four things: continue to learn about the realms and In-Between by finding more tranquil souls to hang out with; to find time to interview the neighbors about blue cars and the night of Niko's and Angelica's hit and run; how to help Reggie find his ex-wife's and child's killer– possibly his own killer— I couldn't help thinking they were one and the same; and finding time to talk to Tia about family stuff by circumventing the fact that I had snooped through her stuff.

Reggie's case was complicated, and oftentimes when Tia came home from long hours of work, I was at the dinner table, poring over police procedure handbooks instead of working on my homework. Reggie would never have seen the scene of the crime, meaning any chance of finding clues there was useless. He'd been interrogated by the police but had found out nothing besides him being the primary suspect. He'd gone to the morgue, to identify the bodies, but I didn't think we'd find clues there.

The next time I saw Reggie I asked point blank if he had any inkling of his killer, if he'd seen or smelled something in particular before his smothering. Reggie shook his head. I asked tentatively if he could show me his memory of death, but a haunted look came into his eyes.

"I wouldn't recommend it. It would be mighty unpleasant for you."

"How?"

He bit his lip but didn't respond.

"Dang it! How? Answer my question," I said, sliding as the ship rolled and tossed under us. It was a tumultuous day in the In-Between.

Reggie looked at me again, then gestured to me, pointing to the deck. Sighing, I lugged over the wash basin I brought every time now and dumped it. The deck pitched, and I tumbled forward, Reggie jumping in behind me.

At first, I thought we'd made a mistake. That we ended up in the wrong realm or something. Everything was pitch black, silent. It took a moment to realize I was laying in bed. Reggie sunk into me, his ghost form replicating his memory.

He'd been sleeping. I didn't get a chance to look at his surroundings before a darkness descended on my face. Reggie thrashed, twisting and turning violently. But the darkness persisted and pressed heavier and heavier.

The strangest sensation came over me. It felt like I should be choking too, but I was stuck in a simulacra of the act. Reggie's panic and despair started to invade me, as his movements became more frenetic. I forced myself to look for anything that could help, but I could discern nothing besides that darn darkness. Just a heavy breathing. I listened vainly for other auditory clues, like heel sounds or jangling of jewelry, but this killer was frustratingly quiet.

Reggie's movements started to slow, and his ghost form gasped, his throat rattling, his windmilling arms flailing feebly. This couldn't be good. Even as a ghost reliving this memory had to be a living hell. What was I thinking? Even if there were clues here, there had to be another way. Not through seeing his gruesome death.

Stop, I thought clear as a gong, and we catapulted out of the memory, back onto the steamship deck. Reggie and I didn't speak at first. I broke the silence once my heart stopped pounding. Grief and guilt flooded me, making my words stutter.

"I am so sorry. I should have listened to you."

He righted himself and shrugged. "I warned you. But you had to find out for yourself."

I was grateful that his tone wasn't accusatory. Even bringing up past trauma to a ghost doesn't make it all right. It took a few moments for me to organize my thoughts.

"Are there any other memories that could give us clues as to your killer? Or your ex and daughter's killer?"

Reggie pondered, angling his body toward the tempestuous sea. "All I've got is my own research and going to my ex's lover's houses." He bowed his head apologetically. "Yes, I stalked some of them. She kept the worst company." A frown passed over his ruddy face. "I don't think there's anything else."

I rubbed my hands over my face. "That's a start."

We agreed to meet up as soon as I had time to start with his memories to write down the addresses and phone numbers he knew of his ex's.

***

I craved a break from all this supernatural business, and

Reggie's death had left me more perturbed than I wanted to admit. It was one thing to read about murder. It was another to see it happen and being incapable of doing anything. It had been a bloodless murder, but also calculated, deliberate and cruel. Not for nothing, I wondered if Reggie's killer was the same as his daughter and wife's, why the sudden change in modus operandi. Why the brutal murder for them, and a less gruesome one for Reggie? I cast my emotions to the side, but not before getting a brief whiff of intuition that the murderer might be male.

My mind worked best when it was preoccupied with other things, the same way I half-ignored the reality around me to get in the In-Between, the same way Tia left all her various pans and pots simmer away on the stove as she prepared an elaborate meal.

I spent afternoons after school focusing on the photos of my family and trying to suss out who was who in the tree. I scoured our house for other clues, other pics, but found none.

I'd bought parchment paper with my own allowance and started to trace a genealogy tree. It had more question marks and random names than anything else. I'd drawn four generations but had no idea where to go from there. I was at the bottom; Tia was up above. But those were the only concrete facts.

I was at my messy desk, colored pens strewn everywhere, ready to pull my hair out, having started a simple macaroni and cheese recipe on the stove, when Tia came home. I was too deep in my thoughts to notice the water was boiling over. The sound of her moving the pot and turning off the burner stirred me out of my mental quandary.

"Cavillaca, honestly. Keep an eye on your food!" She unslung her purse and put it next to her raincoat on the hook in the wall. As always, her purse fell anyway from sheer weight.

"What are you working so hard on anyway? Is it your Spanish?" she asked.

I shook my head. With no small amount of trepidation, I angled my paper toward her, along with the letters, pictures, and my notes.

She approached, her tasseled top brushing against the desk, her dark eyes widening. "You've been going through my stuff again…" she said. "Did you do that all by yourself? Hija…" Her voice choked, a blend of pride, disbelief and anger coarsening her voice.

"There is so much I don't know, Tia. Where I come from. Who our family is. There are so many names. Who are Manuela, Jose, Eduardo, Gloria, Pablo, Camilla, and Dolores? Why did they decide to come to the US? Also, I didn't know you traveled so much in the US!"

Tia flinched and sat heavily across from me, her mass of dark hair flecked with gray moving forward, hiding her face from view.

"Hija, there is so much you don't know. It is my fault. It is all my fault…"

She started to sob, pitching her face in her hands, tears dribbling between her fingers. I stared at her, a sick feeling growing in my stomach.

"Tia. What are you talking about?"

Tia sniffed and shook her head, trying to hold herself together. Between her stammering and tears, the truth poured out.

"Cavillaca, first you need to understand that the world is much more complex, dangerous, and magical than you think. You know that I believe in the old gods, and I used to practice white magic. I was a bruja."

I raised my eyebrows. I had not realized that last part.

"Our family is vast. Generations of generations of our ancestors come from our native Peru."

"Do we come from Ollantaytambo?" I asked, pushing my notes toward her.

She nodded. "Some of the more recent generations have moved to Chinchero."

She paused delicately touching the stack of letters on my desk. My various school trophies and eclectic knickknacks from local art shows and fairs seemed tiny and faded compared to her presence. A crackling energy radiated off her.

"These are letters that chronicle some of your grandparents' travels to the United States and Europe. They were born in 1921, and life became hard for them. They searched for better opportunities. We have the brujeria in our family. Most of us practiced white magic. Some of us turned to black magic. It called unwarranted attention on us."

Shaking, Tia glanced at the pictures, sorrow lacing her voice.

"My generation was born. We spent our time between our homeland and Europe. We tried to forget our past, our witchcraft. My sister, my brother and I dabbled with it, but our parents would get so angry. So, we stopped. For a time. Meanwhile, other members of our family started to have the worst bad luck: dying from stupid accidents, losing their spouses at sea, succumbing to the worst kinds of cancer. After our seventeen great grandparents died within five years of each other, we knew we must have upset the gods. We tried to keep hidden, mind our business."

I leaned forward, knocking over some of my trophies and knickknacks, rustling the papers surrounding us. Tia flinched and continued.

"We lost sight of our cousins after a time. Our parents took no chances. My mother thought we should move somewhere else. Forsake Europe and Peru entirely. But dad didn't want to. Peru was our home. My sister and I, we kept our heads down, letting go of our magic. Our brother on the other hand… Headstrong, proud, he didn't want to renounce his heritage, so he dabbled deeper into white and black magic. He went out on pilgrimages, seeking to commune with the gods all over Latin America. One day…" She hesitated, looking at me to make sure I was still listening. "One day, he went deep into the rainforest and met some magical spirits. They played with him and deceived him, but he overcame them. My brother wasn't dumb. But he got too cocky, went deeper into the forest. He fell on Chullachaki. He got too arrogant and came way too close. The creature attacked him and put him under a spell. I don't know what happened during that time. But when my brother came back, he wasn't the same. Half crazed, he kept mumbling that our family had attracted the attention of the gods and to beware. He became like an animal, pacing around the house, locking himself in the bedroom and having fits for nights and days on end. He kept repeating the same thing when he remembered to talk like a human. He said Chullachaki required an offering. A baby in return for his sanity. A special baby with powers."

Tia shuddered, clasping her arms, suddenly looking girlish and frail.

"I didn't know he was serious. Nor that he was looking at babies from our own family at first. He hunted for our cousins, to reunite the family he said. But he came back empty-handed and surlier than before. Not the right ones, he said, twitching and drooling like a bloodhound on a trail. We were stupid enough to dismiss his words as lunatic ravings. My sister… my precious sister had given birth to you. How I remember her joy, her pride, when she had you." Tia looked at me fondly, her dark eyes shining with wetness.

"Your father was out bartering, a simple paisano proud to work with his hands. He did basket weaving and sold his wares every weekend. He was not there when she gave birth, but as soon as word spread, he dashed home. We all lived at my mother's house then."

A sense of foreboding made my skin crawl. The smell of burning food filled the house, but I couldn't be bothered to open a window.

"Your uncle got to meet you; it was only normal. He lived in the house too, and we didn't think… We didn't think, that's all."

Tia wiped her eyes angrily. She tried to gaze at me, but it skittered away, her shame driving her to look anywhere else.

"He was the most helpful uncle. He offered to watch over you, he helped your parents with errands, he even tried to sing songs to you. However… his fits became worse. We ended up having to lock him in his room and ask for help from the local shamans. We didn't dare use our magic to try to help him. None of their remedies worked. He was too cursed. One night… your mother awoke to find you gone. Your parents immediately set out to find you. For seven nights and seven days, I waited for them to come back. I knew a dark fate had befallen them."

Sobbing threatened to consume her once more, but Tia took some deep breaths to calm herself down.

"I set on their trail. I even used my white magic to follow them. Eventually, I found their bodies. Your parents, dead in the rainforest, the land scuffed and burned around them. My sweet sister and husband, dead by my brother's hand. I managed to find him. He had you in his arms, his mind completely gone. I tried to reason with him. But he wouldn't let you go. He kept screaming it was necessary. He'd had visions that you were the key. I couldn't encourage his madness. I fought him. My own brother. I overpowered him, but I couldn't kill him." Tia hiccupped, reining in her sorrow. "I took you, Cavilla, and I ran, as hard as I could, abandoning our family home. I went to Europe, but he followed me there. I went to the US; he followed me there too. I prayed to the gods for him to leave me alone, that one day or another, whatever debt our family owed, whatever insult we'd inadvertently lent to the gods, would be paid back. I came to Florida, at my wits' end. You were a tiny baby girl then. You became incredibly sick. Almost in a coma-like state. I tended to you best I could. I thought you were dying. Then, one morning, you woke up and everything was fine. But any lingering magic I still had was gone. And from there, my brother hasn't bothered us."

I opened my mouth, so many more questions ready to fall out. But the weight of it all threatened to squeeze the breath from my body. For someone who'd had just been my Tia my entire life, to know there was so much more out there, made my head spin. And my mom had been Tia's sister. My parents… both dead because of my uncle. Tia's brother, mind broken because of whatever tomfoolery he'd done with a demon. It was unfair. It was like a horrible joke.

"That's why I don't like to say names out loud. They have power. Even without my magic… I don't want to take risks. I don't want to attract any more attention to our family than we already have. Cavilla, I understand you want to know where you come from. But while my brother is alive, you are still in danger. I can't share anything too detailed with you until he passes. To be honest, I never wanted you to find this out. You would have been happier not knowing any of this." She started to take the letters and photos, pulling them toward her.

A bubble of anger formed inside me. It made my words come out squeaky and wrong. "So, we are to be isolated from our own family until he dies? We have to live the rest of our lives in fear? What do you mean you didn't want me to find out? It's *my* family too! I deserve to know about our past, no matter how painful it is. My parents are dead. I don't even know their names," I wheezed, grief strangling me. "It's not your place to withhold information from me. I have a right to know."

"Cavilla, I was just trying to protect you. Everything I did was to protect you," Tia said, frowning.

"It doesn't make sense. My passport only has one trip in it, from Peru to Florida. That's it," I said, narrowing my eyes at her.

Tia blushed. "I am so sorry. I had your passport modified, so you would never suspect. Better to believe you had an uneventful life than to see trips I couldn't explain. I never wanted to outright lie to you. I have a friend who helped cover our tracks on the legal side. Can't you see—"

I exploded. "You did everything you could but lie outright! I'm not sure you were protecting me so much as saving face. Your brother did this. You couldn't even kill him? After he killed your sister, and her husband? You think withholding information from me would solve anything? And you still want to keep doing it? Like I can't handle the truth?"

I leapt from the chair, walking to and fro, my words spilling out faster and faster.

"You have no idea what I can handle. I have been able to access the realm of the dead for months and months now. I talk to the dead. They come to me. I help them. I even figured out how to access hanan pacha and uku pacha. I handle death all the time."

Tia's face drained of color. Her mouth worked, but she couldn't speak.

"I want you to tell me the truth. Give me names. Besides, I think I figured it out. My mom's name. It was Celestina, wasn't it?"

Tia nodded, horror on her face.

"What was my father's name?"

She shook her head. "We don't want to draw attention…" she said feebly.

"What was his name? Tell me!"

She bowed her head. "Ramon. Ramon Valdez."

My chest heaved, my mind anchoring their names in my soul. Tia stirred, as she tried to make sense of what I had said.

"If they are dead, surely they are in hanan pacha. I can find them. Maybe I can find out more stuff." I paused. "And you had my passport modified too? Isn't that illegal?"

Tia waved her hands, dismissing my last concern. Her eyes

fixed me with a terror I couldn't ignore despite my rage.

"What is this about accessing the pachas, going into the realm of the dead? Stop lying child. You've never dealt with magic, thank the gods, your overactive imagination is at it again."

Her jewelry trembled as she tried to still her hands from their intermittent quaking.

"I am not lying," I said frigidly, "and I've been able to see the dead for months now. Remember Angelica and Niko? Well, they come to see me all the time. I've helped Mr. Jackson cross the other side. And there's many more in the In-Between. I don't know how to help them all leave, but I will figure it out. There's this place, this steamship; Rumba guides me there, but she's actually Ai-Apaec too. There are these boiler rooms, which lead to hanan and uku pacha. I can access them, Tia. It seems I'm the only one who can—"

"Stop lying, child!" Tia screamed, getting up and pointing a finger at me. Her red fingernail polish seemed to dart like a barb into my heart. "Magic of that level doesn't exist. You can't access magic. You're imagining things to deal with your grief. I need to take you to the school counselor if it's that bad. You need to stop reading about our gods –"

"No. You wouldn't. Adding a counselor would only dig deeper in our family's business. Also, just because you lost your magic doesn't mean I don't have any," I said quietly, clenching my fists. "Just because you can't see it doesn't mean it's not real. Have I ever lied to you? That's rich coming from the woman who tried to erase all trace of our family because of magical monsters or something. Speaking of which," I leaned and gathered the swath of letters and pictures across from me, "these are mine."

Tia gasped and fumbled at my hands, but I deftly gathered the documents close.

"You had no right to keep this from me. If you wanted to protect me, you would have warned me of the danger surrounding our family. You called me a gringa all these years, and even if it was a joke, it was cruel. Cruel, because you stamped down a part of my heritage knowingly. If there truly is danger, I will find the answers and I will walk into it with my eyes wide open."

I walked away from her, and she yelled after me.

"Cavillaca! Stop, hija, basta por favor! You don't know what you're talking about. If you can truly access the pachas, you are in danger. He will find you! If you have this power you speak of, you will be a walking target for–"

I slammed my bedroom door so hard the medals on my wall fell to the floor.

***

I stormed through our neighborhood, the town lights flickering their ghostly orange glow over the cracked sidewalks. The stars glimmered softly above, and I hated their beauty. Everything was deceit, everything was confusion. All of Tia's weird behavior made sense now. A part of me knew she hadn't meant any harm. But dang, she'd chosen the worst way to go about protecting me. It hadn't been her choice to make. Withholding information was never the answer. If she knew me well enough, she'd know that I would suss out a secret in no time. She'd accused me of lying about my power. Did my Tia ever actually know me? Had she crafted a false image of me all these years?

I sat on the curb, gasping as mixed emotions threatened to choke me. It was too much. Of all people, I hadn't expected Tia to be keeping things from me. If her story was true, I was in danger. My uncle could come after me. If I had any sense, I would stop going into the In-Between, at least for a while. That explained Rumba's protective behavior too. She'd known.

But I was just coming into my power, whatever it was. I wasn't going to let go. I had Reggie to help, Niko and Angelica. And many more. If my uncle wanted to come after me, let him. In my current state, if he walked to me right now with all his scary magic, I'd punch him right out.

As my thoughts whirred angrily, I vaguely heard a disturbance two houses down. An older voice and a young voice arguing, then I heard a car going by. A streak of blue flashed across my vision, and I reminded myself I was here to investigate, not to wallow in my self-pity. I recalled the houses that had blue vehicles parked in their yard when I'd been in the In-Between with my friends. The Capidaglis and Mrs. Peloza. I got up, sucking in the impending tears, and checked to see if there was light at the Capidaglis' house. There was, and I heard their TV. I knocked on the door, very aware it was nine at night. Thankfully, no resentment crinkled her face as Mrs. Capidagli answered the door.

"Cavilla. How are you? Are you all right? Come in, come have a tea or coffee."

"No thank you, Mrs. Capidagli. I just wanted to ask a few questions. It's related to Angelica and Niko. Did you hear anything the night of the hit and run? December the twelfth 1995? See anything?"

She shook her head sorrowfully, a wave of lilac scented essence floated in the air.

"Sorry, Cavilla. Same thing I told the police. I can't hear, especially when there is background noise. Even with my hearing aid." She pointed to her ear with the device.

I nodded and asked, "Did anyone ever use your blue SUV? Was the car here the night of that accident?"

She frowned, pursing her lips, but my instincts screamed that I was wasting my time. I couldn't explain it. But the answer wasn't here.

"No," she said after a while. "I can't say for sure, but Carl was out visiting his father during that time. He was the only one to use it. He was in Mississippi that night. Right, honey?" she asked the old man sitting on the couch.

"Yes," he called, lowering the TV volume.

"Sorry, we're of no more help," she said.

"It's all right. Thank you anyway."

"You sure you don't want a coffee or tea?"

"Yes."

"Okay. Give our greetings to your aunt."

I closed the door with no further ado. I decided since I was on a roll to walk the strip and ask other neighbors, the ones who had dashcams, if their footage had captured anything.

I went to four houses, each more luscious than the last. One didn't answer. Two let me in, and showed me their footage from that night, impressed I'd thought of looking at their footage, while also embarrassed they hadn't thought of it. But the footage was too grainy to be helpful and at the wrong angle. The last house I went to, the resident admitted they didn't keep their footage from that far back.

That left going to Mrs. Peloza's house, the other one with the blue vehicle. On my way there however, my phone rang. It was Tia. I let it ring, letting the chill of the night also wrap around my heart. The cringey ringtone rang through the night. I made it to my neighbors' garden, the dew from the grass making my sneakers slip and I paused. Stupid and cruel as I thought her actions to be, she was still my Tia. My only family. Well, the only family here with me. Who knew if one day I would ever meet the other members of the family, assuming they were alive, and unaffected by the apparent curse from the gods.

I breathed out. Mrs. Peloza's house was dark now. It was 10:43p.m. I didn't want to bug her. I'd come back later.

I walked slowly home, dragging my feet. Tia sat on the couch but I avoided her gaze. I ignored the cup of hot chocolate she'd left for me on the dining table. Going straight to my room, I practiced my clarinet, until my breath was ragged, and until my fingers couldn't support the clarinet anymore.

7

A PARADOXICAL MAN

After that, I made my best effort to go more often and as long as possible into the In-Between. Reality and I weren't on speaking terms, so I used that time to focus on Reggie. He took me into his non-traumatic memories first, showing me when his daughter came over: a little slip of a girl, with red hair that refused to stay in its pigtails and perpetually skinned knees. She loved to roller skate on the street, and work with her hands, crafting objects in the backyard. But Lauren had also inherited her father's love of the sea. I stood ankle deep in sea water as Reggie explained to her in his memory how to surf on their once-a-year trip to California, how to observe the wave. I let myself be sucked into those joy-filled, sunny afternoons, mirroring Reggie's pose on his surfboard, pride tugging at his lips as he watched his daughter attempt to master surfing.

Afternoons came and went, clouds roiled across the sky in a frantic timelapse of his soul, and the slow descent into depression commenced. Lauren asked him to stop going to the beach. She hunkered down at his home on the sofa, playing card games and discarding them. She looked out the window, spooked by the slightest noise, running to the sofa and burrowing in the cushions.

She'd never been one for hugs. But her silence and loneliness grew a barrier of unsaid hurt and isolation between herself and Reggie.

Reggie wanted to show me his ensuing memories, the memories that came after their death. I refused at first. It was all quickly becoming overwhelming. But then again, I'd pushed him to show me his memory of dying. If he could withstand it, so could I endure the painful memories preceding his death.

We jumped into his memory together, of him being woken up at ten in the morning, jostled from his solitary breakfast of a stale croissant, cold coffee, and a cigarette by policemen. With hostility in their eyes and looming postures, they asked him where he'd been the night before.

Reggie answered honestly saying," I am an insomniac and was out taking a walk in the neighborhood to clear my head."

The squad of policemen shook their heads or gave meaningful looks, angling forward more, threatening him as they stood on his wooden verandah, decorated with chintzy gnomes and rusty pinwheels, half dying plants, and empty pots. It had been a clear blue morning, not a cloud in sight, not a whiff of wind. No one expected to get bad news on a morning like that.

Reggie braced himself (and so did I, standing literally in his shoes), as they dropped the sordid news that his wife and child had been found dead in the woods. His answers and pleading became quiet static noises, interspersed with incredulous gurgles.

"They were clearly murdered," a policeman said, "major contusions, bruising. Their faces are barely recognizable…"

Another one asked, "Did anyone see you on your walk last night?"

Reggie shook his head, not knowing, not remembering. One of the younger policemen tsked, and said, "You had no love for your wife. We should have known after the number of calls we got from her complaining about you. She should have gotten a restraining order. Maybe then she wouldn't be dead."

Reggie's hat slipped to the ground. They'd had their share of explosive arguments, yes. Gotten almost to the point of being physical with each other, yes. He and Dalea both had anger issues they'd never worked to resolve. A few heated phone calls to the police during drunken arguments, yes had happened. But never anything beyond that. As he struggled to form his thoughts into sentences that didn't incriminate him, the younger policeman resumed speaking.

"We're waiting on that coroner's report. But the way they were beaten up. Must have been a mighty wicked weapon. You have a wood workshop," he said staring at the side of the house. "Maybe we should take a look in there and see if anything matches up, hmm?"

Reggie finally managed to croak out, "You need a warrant for that."

An older, squat policeman nodded. "We can't search the house yet. But we do need to take you in for questioning. I'm sorry. You are her ex-husband and with your past… We need to make sure."

Reggie followed them to the car blindly, his movements stiff and labored. His mind whirred, not understanding. Lauren and Dalea both dead? Murdered brutally? How? By whom? And he was a suspect. That was they were taking him in. They actually thought he was the murderer. The numbness took him as he was escorted to the police car and to the station.

The ghost form of Reggie paused the memory. Or was it me? I didn't see the utility of seeing his interrogation with the police. We both knew he hadn't done it.

"Do you need to see where I identify their bodies?" Reggie asked, his sad dark eyes the same color as his cap. "It's a few days after the police took me in and let me go."

I thought about it, my body half in and out of the car, my form translucent as it mimicked Reggie's body. The sun shone so brightly it was almost cruel. A warm presence in Reggie's world of incredulity and frozen horror. Looking at the bodies might give a clue as to how they died, perhaps a psychological insight into the murderer. But to my great shame, I didn't know much about forensics and weapons, much less what kind of marks specific weapons made. I vowed to look into that as soon as possible when I left the In-Between. The information that would be helpful would all be in the coroner's report and/or the police report. Alas, that was not information Reggie would have access to.

But could I hope to solve his case if I chose to ignore potential clues? Anything could help lead us in the direction of the murderer. I could perhaps glean some information from his conversation with the pathologist and diener. I told Reggie that I wanted to see the memory of him talking with the pathologist and diener, but not the viewing of the bodies. He relaxed a little and took my hand. I clasped it, and we materialized in the pathologist's office. I/Reggie sat across from the pathologist and his assistant. The ghost form of Reggie melted into the shadows of the room, distancing himself from his own memory. I focused on the conversation happening. Though, as Reggie's brain was still in complete distress, certain words and phrases were cut off or muted.

"Your ex-wife… as you saw… contusions everywhere. Your daughter too… she died quickly. Wife was raped before she died. Did your wife have enemies?"

More static in his mind. It was frustrating inhabiting his body and being limited by it. I stared at the kind faces of the men across from him. Their lips moved, but nothing quite made sense. What stood out, more than the glint of the gold horn-rimmed glasses of the pathologist, or the silver flash of the badges they wore, was a smell. A thick smell of formaldehyde and Vick's vapor rub blended in a gut roiling combination. Another smell wriggled at the edges of awareness: a pungent smell, like a fragrance oil that's been used so often even the walls remembered it. A faint smell of something flowery.

A knock on the door. The funeral director poked his head in and nodded at Reggie.

"Sorry sir, but we need to see you after you're done here."

A few more minutes of static and Reggie/I went to meet the funeral director.

"What arrangements do you want for your wife and daughter?"

"Ex-wife," Reggie said out of habit.

"Yes, well. Did she leave a will?"

"No. I don't think so." Reggie said, rubbing a hand through

his salt and pepper hair.

He started to cry, overwhelmed by it all. The director hovered awkwardly, waiting for him to finish. The diener who'd come out of the previous room put a hand on Reggie's shoulder.

"If you need grief counseling, we have people available…"

The memory darkened, and it felt like reality unspooled away from me, yanking out of my grip. As the deck of the In-Between steamship materialized, I gazed at Reggie. He spread his hands apologetically.

"Sorry," he said in his deep voice made huskier by his smoking. "It's a lot. Seeing it with you helps a bit. But I really want to find the bastard who –"

"I know," I cut in, wishing I could just siphon his pain away. "That's why I'm here. We will find answers."

We sat on the deck silently until Reggie broke the silence.

"Dalea had no will. Like everything else, she didn't think it through. None of her ex-boyfriends showed up to help. I told the mortician that she probably would have liked a Christian burial and Mass. But I can't be sure. She was a damn enigma, always changing her mind. None of her ex-boyfriends even showed up at her funeral. No classmates of Lauren's showed up either. It's like… like they died in absolute loneliness."

I let him talk, jangling my bracelet, its rough texture soothing as it rubbed back and forth on my fingertips. He needed to let out all his grief.

"The rape made me think a boyfriend did it. I'm just glad he didn't touch Lauren. My precious, my darling… Though she wasn't the same…I told you that already." Reggie sucked in a breath and grabbed his pant legs, seizing the widest part of his jean hem.

"I tried to tell them my gut feelings, but no one listened. I was lucky to even be free. Of course, it's always the ex-husband who's the guilty one… I just wish… I hadn't seen their bodies. Seeing their dead corpse wasn't a relief. It wasn't a way to say goodbye. I was just horrified. Dead bodies are so different. Dalea had a sharp beauty to her, if you could look past her constant shrewish frown and words. Lauren, sweet baby, you saw her. She was going to grow up to be the best of us. That red hair, like my grandmother's… Well, poor thing was bruised and swollen so much I couldn't see her face. All that I recognized was her hair. Dalea… it was even worse. Yes, they were pummeled. The mortician tried to spare my eyes." Reggie laughed bitterly. "The damage was so bad nothing was covering *that* up."

We sat quietly again, his laugh swallowed by the roaring sea around us. Even the other dead gave us a wide berth. After what felt like hours, Reggie sighed.

"You'd think a woman who cheated on you, and then accused you of cheating to divorce you would slink away from the affections of my heart. But no. A part of me still loved her. A scornful love, yes. Some days, just dropping off Lauren at her place took too much out of me. Seeing her was pain sometimes. Seeing her dead was a shadow of that pain. Why is that?"

"She was still your child's mother," I ventured. "No matter how much she wronged you she didn't deserve to die like that. No one deserves to die like that."

I didn't care if she'd cheated on him twenty times, being beaten like an animal wasn't a good karmic payback. Looking at Reggie, some of his zest for vengeance seeped into me; the deadly resolve in his eyes, the aggressive tilt of his chin, despite the depression that permeated his every limb, his every facial expression.

"Let's catch that son of a bitch," I said.

***

Reggie led me to memories of him investigating his family's death. Many memories started off the same, him slumped over a desk in his office, surrounded by bookshelves sagging with the weight of his tomes. Gaudy lamps from different time periods that didn't go well together perched on incongruous spaces on his multiple desks. Those desks he's crafted and polished himself. Many of the desks held intricate designs and carvings so elaborate and small I knew he'd spent weeks working on them. Every desk had a specific stain and polish depending on what he used it for.

Open books with bookmarks jutting out from bent pages littered his desks. Most were poetry and reference books. I tried to see more into Reggie's psyche, but his memory form compelled me to concentrate on what he was working on. Writing down addresses and phone numbers. At first, I stared dumbly, not knowing what it was. Then it dawned on me, previous memories of conversations with Reggie coming to the surface.

"This is it. The addresses of the people you suspected. All her exes. Her current boyfriends too."

Ghost Reggie nodded, leaning away from the half-finished sled that stood in the middle of his office.

I paused the memory this time, thinking of a slight snag in the loop of this memory. I caught it and arrested the flow of time. Ironic, since we were already in a stasis of reality and time.

"How do you have this information?"

"I…" he bowed his head, a slight blush creeping under his sloppy shave job. "I swiped her address book one night and memorized them. I have a great memory. It's how I used to do my poetry readings on the fly back in the day…" He trailed off. "I think she found out. I wasn't allowed back in her house for a while. Not that it mattered. I made a copy of her key. She never knew."

"Reggie!" I said, aghast. "Your stalker behavior just gets worse and worse. You were that jealous of her? After she cheated on you?"

Needless to say, not that I'd been interested in dating, but Reggie and Dalea's relationship gave me all the incentive needed to stay away from so-called romantic affairs.

"Yes," he said simply. "I know it wasn't a good thing. I wasn't the best man around her. She was right about that. If you think that's terrible, I also stalked her boyfriends. I have memories of that I can show you. I hope it will help. I hope my bad behavior can help catch a murderer." His expression hardened.

Reggie da Costa. I don't think I'd have liked him much in real life. Certainly not around his wife. But he'd been a different man with Lauren. I'd seen it with my own eyes. Teaching her to surf, letting her run around in the neighborhood with some of her friends. Watching TV with her and gifting her wooden carvings she asked him to make. Sometimes, he'd read her poetry before going to sleep.

He was disorganized, yet purposeful. Deeply caring yet burning with a thirst for revenge. Reggie was full of paradoxes. And he needed my help. Even though I didn't endorse his behavior, hopefully like he said, it would prove beneficial to our search. Private investigators sometimes got their hands a *little* dirty every now and then. According to the stories I read anyway. You had to be willing to bend the rules somewhat.

The half-finished sleigh caught my eye. "Why do you have that?"

"To remind me I make mistakes."

We both laughed.

***

My next few days bounced back and forth between shamelessly stalking Reggie's ex-wife's boyfriends and poring over the letters I'd kept after my argument with Tia. Even as my attention was riveted on clues, as Reggie showed me his memories of hiding in bushes or sitting in his car across the street, observing one of Dalea's beaus, so was my attention distracted by those letters. What would happen if I took those letters with me in the In-Between? Since I couldn't get information out from Tia, perhaps the In-Between might yield something.

One evening, I toyed with the letters, playing with their flimsiness, smelling the musty odor that emanated from them. The light became a half-shadow of itself, snaking shamelessly into my room like it was wont to do. Angelica and Niko materialized into being, already beaming with news they wanted to tell me. The half-light touched the letters and a golden spark flared around the words, around the pictures, coiling and shimmering devilishly. The light crept around my fingers, tickling them with the flame of knowledge. Yes, I had brought the letters to the In-Between. I was certain now there would be something unlocked.

I shook the letters waiting and wanting to see more happen, but the light dimmed and flickered to a low beam slinking along the paper.

Niko asked, "What is that?"

"I think this is the key to help me find my family," I said hardly believing it was real.

As I made that mental side-step into the intersections of reality and magic, slitting my eyes, which I knew wasn't necessary, but it helped me do it better, or so it felt, the pathway to my bathroom and the In-Between opened. Rumba walked out of the pathway toward me, tail high in the air. I was surprised. She didn't often come into my bedroom anymore. She mostly stayed on the steamship calmly supervising me, like a godly chaperone. Her cool green eyes regarded me, her tail swishing.

"Be careful with those," she said in her dual voice.

I was too excited to pay attention. I gathered Niko and Angelica in my arms, their wispy forms breaking apart.

"Come! I think I'm finally going to get some answers."

I dashed onto the path, them closely behind. I emerged onto the deck, nearly tumbling as the steamship pitched and rolled violently. The letters flared to life in my hand, gold and white threads of light interlacing and forming geometrical shapes. They solidified as a prism over my heart. A gleaming trail of glyphs emerged on the deck, leading to the cabin. Without checking to see if my friends or Rumba were following, I dashed into the cabin and down the staircase. The trail of light flared brighter and brighter as I followed it, sparks flying up my jeans, floating and dancing in the air. The trail ended at the two heavy boiler room doors, the glittering lines of light angling sharply in the crack at the bottom of the doors.

I paused. Why did the trail lead me to two different paths? That didn't make sense.

Rumba materialized out of nowhere, her paws treading the pathways. She meowed plaintively, setting herself between the two doors. I tried to step around her, but every time, she adjusted, barely moving as she did so. In frustration, I stomped my foot.

"Can you get out of my way please?" Answers, finally some answers waited behind those doors, I was sure. Why they led into hanan and uku pacha I wasn't one hundred percent certain. The important part was that I knew where to go now. Years' worth of mystery would finally be solved.

Rumba hissed at me, and I stopped in shock.

"It is not the right time," she said, staring at me deeply.

I crossed my arms. "Says you. Look at this. It's literally leading me to the places I will find answers."

She shook her head. "It does. But it is still not the right time for you to find out. Keep those letters close. You will know when it is time."

I started to quiver. I was so tired of enigmas surrounding me. I wanted answers. Even in this realm where I had powers no one dreamed of, I still was mostly in the dark. It wasn't fair.

"When will I know when the time is right then? A sign in the sky? A message? What?" I shouted.

But she stared at me impassively.

"You keep assuming I'll know what to do. I'm guessing here! What if I make a mistake? People are relying on me. I can't let them down. It's fine and all to solve other peoples' problems, but what about mine, huh? No one seems to care."

I started to cry, hunching over, trying to stem the tears. The words were bratty, I knew it as soon as they flew out of my mouth. I couldn't help it. It was all becoming too much. What use was it to have otherworldly powers if you were confused all the time?

Rumba butted her head against my legs firmly, making it so I had to bend down and scoop her up. She started to purr, her feline vibration magnified in the salty gloom.

"You are not ready yet. Very soon. You will be. Wait for now. I promise you will know. If you go now, you will be too vulnerable. Don't brand a painted target on your back, child."

"Is this about my murderous uncle?" I sobbed, clutching her tighter.

She nodded, and I stormily continued to cry. The letters crinkled on my chest; her fur tickled my nose. Through it all, the glowing lines to the doors thrummed, waiting for me.

I had to let it go.

8

MORAL CONFLICT

I kept my word, securing the letters in my bedroom, waiting for a darn sign. In a huff, I pulled over my chemistry homework, ignoring my journal where I'd just chronicled my impressions of Reggie's stalking. This week we'd gone to six exes of his wife's. We'd gone from trailer parks, to bungalows, to a nice two story house in the suburbs. Some of the guys had looked perfectly decent and correct despite Reggie's grumblings. We'd also visited memories of him stalking Dalea's house, waiting for her boyfriends to come out. A couple looked sleazy, indeed; one smelled of pizza grease. The other looked like a homeless person, completely shaggy and unkempt. Sometimes, we saw Lauren too, trying to stay out of the way. I paid special attention to the memories where the girl looked spooked. I'd noted the names in my journal: Javier Desantos. Mel Smaller. Robert Bello. They were frequent visitors.

The last memory I'd accompanied Reggie on was one of him hiding in the bushes, listening to a conversation between Dalea and Robert. They'd been talking about moving in together, but Dalea was worried it would perturb Lauren. Robert thought Lauren didn't like him, but she'd get over it. I didn't like Robert's high pitched tone, or the way he slung mud at Reggie as Dalea talked about him. But none of it screamed murder. None of the conversations or behaviors we'd observed had given any definitive clues.

I circled the molecular diagrams on my homework aimlessly. The lesson was boring. I'd nearly fallen asleep during the lecture. Even looking at the textbook didn't help. I cracked my knuckles. Screw it, I would come back to it. It was 5:45. Tia wouldn't be home for another hour and a half. I might as well take a walk to clear my head.

I wrapped a scarf around my neck and started my usual circular tour of the neighborhood. Some kids were in their backyard, jumping on their trampoline. A dog barked in the distance. Mr. Corrida was mowing his lawn. That was unusual for him. Dimly, I heard party noise at the Smiths' house. Oh yes, Olivia was turning sixteen. I used to go over to her place when we were younger. But after a while she said I was too creepy and refused to invite me afterward. That had been during my emo phase, when I'd talked non-stop about death, before I'd discovered murder mysteries and particularly Agatha Christie, channeling my obsession into something more acceptable.

I passed by Mrs. Peloza's house and saw the back of a blue car. My memory of that afternoon with Angelica and Niko jumped to the forefront. A blue car! She was the only one I had yet to interrogate about that night of the hit and run. I stepped in her driveway, past the flattened flower beds, past the deflated basketballs and rusty basketball hoop placed haphazardly in front of the garage. It wasn't a blue car; it was a blue Jeep. Some stickers adorned the bottom part, and a custom chrome grill overlay shone brightly. I turned to the front door and tapped. Some peaceful classical music stopped, then the door opened.

"Hi! Caville, right?" Mrs. Peloza said, blinking blearily through her half-moon glasses.

"Cavilla," I corrected with a smile. "May I come in?"

She hesitated, but let me in. "Do you want a coffee, tea?"

"No thank you. I won't be here long," I said, tying my hair back with the scrunchie I'd brought. A heap of clothing was on the couch, waiting to be folded. Thick sneakers lay by the doorway. Baseball caps hung from a hook by the door. Someone else was here. A man. Or a big teenager.

Mrs. Peloza went in the kitchen and came back with a cold glass of water. She handed it to me, and we hovered awkwardly by the couch. I figured there was no use wasting time.

"Who else is here with you?"

She pinched her lips. "My nephew. He's only here for a few

days."

I glanced around at the house. I saw glimpses of rooms. The two bedrooms I could see were occupied. One overflowed with sportswear, shoes, and sports equipment. In the kitchen, lay a drying rack with multiple plates, glasses, and silverware. I suspected he was staying here for much longer than a few days, but if she lied a little about that, how was it my problem?

"The night of December the twelfth 1995. That was the hit and run that killed Angelica Biou and Niko Gonzalez. Did you see anything in the neighborhood?"

Mrs. Peloza darted to the couch and started to fold the laundry. "No. I go to bed early. The accident happened late at night, didn't it?"

"Yes."

She continued to fold, not meeting my eyes. I glanced at the lava lamps on the dining table, as they changed colors. Something… something wasn't adding up.

"The police report says a blue vehicle hit them. They haven't been able to identify what kind of car it was."

"I don't know what that has to do with me," she said in a clipped tone.

"Is the blue Jeep yours?" I asked. "I've seen it now and again."

Mrs. Peloza hissed as the pile of clothing tumbled to the ground. She threw up her hands and sideways glared at me. "Is now really the time to be talking about this? The accident was two years ago. If the police haven't found anything else, then there is nothing."

I held up my hands defensively. "I was just asking," I said placatingly. "A blue car is pretty unique in our neighborhood. The most common color seems to be white or gray…" I continued with some inane prattle to set her at ease, talking about the models and makes of our neighbors' cars, the new vehicles some had bought, and the effectiveness of their dash cams. I hoped she would take the bait, and say if she had a cam, but she listened passively. Her shoulders relaxed a little, and she progressed through her pile of laundry.

I finished with a statement on how Tia was debating switching out her gray Audi for a sleek yellow BMW. Mrs. Peloza smiled at that and murmured a noncommittal "That's nice."

She glanced at the door, her graying blonde hair unraveling from its curlers. "Well, hope to talk to you again. My nephew will be home soon with the week's groceries." She walked toward the door, holding it open expectantly.

I set down my glass of water and looked at one of the pictures on the dining table. A week's worth of groceries? That sounded like a routine. And she didn't always go to bed early. I'd seen her light on as late as ten or eleven o'clock at night during some of my evening walks.

"I wouldn't mind meeting your nephew, so no worries," I said in response, backing away from the door and lounging against the glass table at the entrance. Tia would have slapped me for my rudeness, justifiably so, but I needed answers. "A week's worth of groceries? Does he usually stay this long? I thought he was only staying for a few days."

Mrs. Peloza blanched, her mouth working. She snapped her silk robe sharply around her, her bony elbows jutting out like a crane. "You're a meddler, aren't you? Please just leave. I don't know what you're hoping to get from this useless conversation."

I launched into a tirade that would have made Tia proud, complete with Spanish curse words interlaced in my dialogue.

"Coño, estoy simplemente pidiendote preguntas innocentas. Unless you have something to hide. What I'm hoping to get? Some closure. For me and my friends. Two of my dearest friends died that night. They died, and they'd just become teenagers. Do you know how hard it is on the parents? Their families haven't been the same since. My friends died from a stupid hit and run. How unfair is it to die like that and not even know who did it? The police gave up, but I haven't. Yes, I'm a meddler. But tell me this: who does the blue Jeep belong to? Answer me this por favor, Mrs. Peloza, and I will leave you alone. That is all I'm asking."

Mrs. Peloza shriveled in her stance like a dying spider. She couldn't meet my eyes. A dead silence permeated her house, but I let it billow and expand. I wasn't intimidated. Stints with the dead in the In-Between made this all a child's game. Finally, she spoke up, in a hallowed voice that forced me to strain to be able to hear.

"The jeep… it is my nephew's. He's the only one who drives it. Yes, he stays with me often. I don't have a choice. He has a hard life." She trailed off, shielding herself from my gaze.

"What happened that night?" I asked softly. "You do remember, don't you?"

"How could I not?" she whispered. "We'd had a terrible argument. I caught him stealing a few things again. He's a raging alcoholic. Part of the reason his parents disowned him. I welcomed him when no one else would. He was just a lost soul. But the alcohol… it consumed him. He was drunk again, I told him he wouldn't be welcome here anymore if he continued to steal. He yelled at me, and he left. It's not until later I learned about your friends. He had a habit of drunk driving. It wasn't hard to connect the dots."

"Yet, you didn't tell anyone," I said numbly, too appalled to yell. All along the answer had been right under my nose. It's always those you suspect the least…

"No. How could I? He has his flaws, my Nicholas, but I couldn't do that to him. His life was already in shambles. He is like a son to me. Yes, he did a terrible thing. I am sorry about your friends. I really am. But to have Nicholas go away for a crime like that. After multiple little felonies he has on his record… It would end his life. I couldn't be responsible for that. If the police didn't find answers, so be it. It was meant to be."

I almost forgot to breathe. If I were in her shoes, maybe, *maybe* I would have done the same. But her nephew did a crime, and a crime needed consequences. My poor friends had died in a hit and run because he was drunk. What a stupid way to die. And he'd avoided legal repercussions, because his aunt was too concerned about the value of his life; she'd made her choice: my friends' lives didn't matter because his was more pathetic. She'd consciously chosen the argument that their death wasn't worth facing the justice system for. She was enabling her nephew in his bad behavior, and in her selfishness to keep him close no matter what, chose to let my friends die shrouded in mystery, with no closure whatsoever. Her nephew was responsible for the hole in my heart not even ghostly Angelica and Niko could fill. My nostrils flared in my quiet rage.

"You lied to the police. I know they questioned everyone in the neighborhood," I seethed. "For all your talk of morals and good Samaritan-ness, you deliberately withheld information to protect Nicholas." His name burned on my tongue. "I'm sorry he's had such a rough time. But he killed my friends and destroyed their family. You were able to hole yourself up here and shield yourself from the world. Nicholas still has his life. Everything is hunky dory for you guys. You're still enabling him. Meanwhile, my friends rot in their graves. Thanks a lot. I don't know how you can look at yourself in the mirror."

I whirled toward her, accidentally knocking her house keys from the ceramic dish she had on the table. I stalked past her, clenching my fists.

"I'm sorry. You've got to understand," she wailed. "He's all I have. Please don't tell anyone. You won't, right, right?" She almost screamed.

I ignored her and headed home, the blood in my ears humming a furious beat.

***

I wanted to reach out to Niko and Angelica so badly. Sadly, I couldn't summon them on command. I'd thought knowing who finally did it would be a satisfying thing, a neat tidy ending that made you feel good. None of Christie's books had prepared me for this.

I paced in my bedroom, avoiding looking at the library shelves full of detective stories. In the books, it almost always ended well. None mentioned the sick feeling churning in my guts. I knew who their killer was, and that he hadn't done it on purpose. Yet, he'd been drunk driving, and it wasn't the first time. Worse, he hadn't confessed afterward and neither had his aunt. They were perfectly willing to keep mum to shelter their lives.

Now I had a dilemma. Obviously, I would tell my friends about this, and hopefully it would help them move on. My heart twisted thinking about my friends being well and truly gone. But what if just the knowledge of it didn't help them move on? My first instinct was to tell the police. Lock up Nicholas and make him pay. Mrs. Peloza's had pleaded with me to not tell anyone. Nevertheless, it should be my duty to expose them. I didn't want to be a tattle tale. Yet, Angie and Niko deserved justice. Also, a point to consider: if I managed to out him, my friends might move on for good. I'd never see them again.

How could I be so selfish? A PI never got emotionally invested. Yet, here I was.

I curled up on the floor, clasping my hands on my head, trying to stem back the flaring headache that erupted. What should I do? As I labored to find the right choice, still feeling ill, it reminded me of my experience living Reggie's death. I felt short of breath, queasy, disoriented. The memory of lying in bed, incapable of doing anything, thrashing around while being smothered… felt similar to what I felt now.

In the blackness behind my eyelids, I re-envisioned the scene. Reggie/me thrashing, incapable of stopping the wielder of the smothering pillow. The grip had been strong. Quite strong, not budging an inch. Reggie was not weak. The killer must have been an athletic man, maybe a body builder of some kind. At least a bigger man than Reggie. And looking back, a scent prickled across my senses, a strange mix of sweat, body odor and a pungent smell of essential oil; much stronger than what I'd smelled at the morgue. An essential oil smell, of a flower. Yes, there had been that smell in Reggie's bedroom when he died. And at the morgue, when we'd looked at the bodies, though much fainter.

I wasn't good with flowers. Tia probably would know; she loved gardening. But as she wasn't here, and we still weren't on the best of terms…

I needed to confirm my theory. Maybe this was just what I needed, a distraction to occupy my brain while I pondered in the background what to do about Nicholas and Mrs. Peloza.

***

I met Reggie and explained my theory.

"We need to revisit the memories of you stalking Dalea's boyfriends. I will observe just the physical aspects of the men, not the conversations this time. Maybe we will get the answers we need." I hefted my notebook, ready to scribble down my observations.

Reggie frowned, thinking it through. "An essential oil smell you say? Dalea sometimes wore perfume and oils."

"Did she wear flowery scents?"

"No. Mostly nuts, like almond, and shea butter. That sort of stuff."

"So the smell I'm detecting has to be the killer!"

"It must be," he said, excitement dancing in his eyes.

"Are you ready?" I asked him, already sloshing the bucket of water on the deck.

He nodded and in we jumped.

I was so intent on my mission the usual disorienting feeling of falling into someone's memory didn't bother me. We methodically went through every memory of his involving seeing a boyfriend of Dalea's. This time, I forced my brain to disassociate a tiny bit, to allow myself some bodily autonomy in his memory so I could scribble notes in my journal. But doing that in someone else's memory was like fighting against riptide.

I added some names and deleted those I'd already put in my journal. I crossed off Javier Desantos and Robert Bello. Mel Smaller stayed on the list, and I added four more names. All were men bigger than Reggie. I kept my nose on the alert, straining against the limitations of being trapped in Reggie's body's memory.

Reggie was about ready to give up when I threw out my hand. We were at Dalea's house, and Lauren was playing in the grass, picking out worms and aligning them to have them race. As soon as the front door opened, and the man called Bob Twindlo stepped out, she gasped and edged back, attempting to hide in a bush of redosier dogwood.

He called out, "Last chance to come with me to the gym, Dalea. You know I don't like an unfit woman. You're getting fat." He turned and his blue gaze halted momentarily on Lauren. She sank further back in the bush.

"It's all right, I'll skip it this time. You know I'm busy. I'm cooking a big meal for us tonight, your favorite," Dalea called, coming to the porch. She fumbled with an apron, her hands shaking.

As she looked at Bob with a mechanical smile, I/Reggie saw the bruise on her cheek. Concealer had been clumsily placed on it, but the bruise still showed. Even ghost Reggie bristled.

"You'd better not mess it up like last time," Bob said in a honeyed voice.

As he exited the backyard and walked close to where I hid behind the fence, a whiff of essential oil hit me. A cloying flowery scent. A gym bag was slung over his toned shoulders. He headed to his car and drove off.

"I think it's him," I mouthed at ghost Reggie who stood next to me. "Take me to other memories of just him."

He obliged, and I observed more conversations but without sound as we were stalking from the car. Dalea and Lauren's body language spoke volumes about their fear of him. At last, we found another memory that was much more helpful: a conversation between Reggie and Bob himself, right outside Dalea's house.

"You're stalking us," Bob said, poking Reggie hard in the chest. "How long did you think you could continue?"

"I am. And I'll do it as long as necessary until I know she is safe. Wait till I tell the police you're beating her up." Reggie huffed, his leather maroon coat flapping sadly in the wind.

"I'm sure," Bob chuckled. "When I tell them about your stalker behavior, and the restraining order you're violating, we'll see who's smiling then."

Reggie flushed. "Stop laying your hands on them. It doesn't make you more of a man."

Bob got in his face, and the cologne he wore washed me in its pungent fragrance; yep, the same flowery smell. "What do you know of being a man? You haven't gotten the girl. And you won't. Dalea is mine. So is Lauren. She knows her daddy is a loser." Bob rubbed his hands together in glee. "Next time I catch you snooping, I will beat you within an inch of your life." He flexed his muscles threateningly.

Bob left Reggie blustering emptily into the dusk, their shadows lengthening on the cracked sidewalks.

I pulled myself out of the memory, forcing Reggie and I to

materialize on the deck of the ship. That had never happened before. My powers were growing.

"That memory was what we needed. He actually threatened you. With that in mind, you didn't think he was the killer?"

Reggie shook his head. "I knew he was a terrible person. But domestic violence doesn't necessarily mean killer."

"I beg to differ," I said.

He looked down in embarrassment. "It's not the first time I've been threatened in my life either. It's a bluster of the moment. I didn't take it seriously."

He hadn't taken it seriously. Yet, all the clues led to the same thing: Bob Twindlo was the murderer. The scent he wore, him being bigger than Reggie and a bodybuilder, and the fact that he beat Dalea was enough proof for me.

The instant the confirmation settled in my gut, a flaring flash of light exploded out from me, a glowing circle with a strange squat figure sporting horns in the middle, which then unraveled and swirled into a mass of golden-reddish lines zigzagging out and laying a path on the deck of the steamship. The aftermath of the initial circular image seared in my eyelids. It was ten times more powerful than when I'd brought my family pictures here. The bright lines laid a trail, just like last time, that went into the ship cabin. I assured Reggie I'd be back.

I went down the staircase. This time, the lines led to the door furthest away, the door that led to uku pacha if I remembered correctly. Why was it leading me there? Then I recalled what I'd been thinking about: Reggie's murderer, Bob Twindlo. That awful flowery smell assaulted my senses, and the lines thrummed as if I'd plucked them. I hesitated, not sure if I was ready for a tryst in this pacha. The last time Rumba had pulled me out. What would going in there do? I thought these doors led to the pachas, realms of the dead. But Bob wasn't dead as far as I knew. Unless he'd had a heart attack or something. *Serves him right*, I thought.

Whatever it was, the path led me here. I had to answer.

I nudged open the door, and the heat made me sweat instantly. The familiar smell of molding water made me gag; fetid streams ran past my feet gurgling like the last breaths of a dying man. The low rumble beat pulsed in the background. Shades of gray, red and brown blended together like the remnants of a scab, painting the multiple tunnels branching skyward in drab tones. I still couldn't see a sky, but the landscape surrounding me had nothing but cave tunnels and entrances climbing up, dizzyingly so. A non-stop drip beat like a metronome came from decaying stalactites as I followed the glowing lines.

"Lead me to Bob Twindlo, wherever he is," I commanded, squinting past the steam forming on the ground. Screams and that working bellows sound laced together to accompany me as I followed the lines. I walked past crumbling tunnels where the dead huddled together, moaning incessantly. I passed forsaken souls, re-enacting murderers they'd done, or trying to shepherd others into puddles ringed with flame. The shrieking and moaning swelled and diminished like an agonized heartbeat.

Finally, the lines stopped at a cave wall with a cascade tumbling down. The water steamed on impact with the ground. I reached forward, focusing on Bob and Reggie's tragedy. The water shimmered and became glossy like a mirror. Vague shapes and shadows acted as a pantomime until the vision cleared. I saw a familiar figure walking to the gym, with an arrogance that shone from every muscle that rolled under the sunlight, every smirk he levied at passerby.

The steam of this place wanted to obscure the scene, but I willed it away, trying to see where Bob was going. He stopped to adjust a missing persons flier on a recycling bin, then he entered his gym. I forced the view to stay on the street with the front of the gym leering at me. Slowly, I shuffled forward, reaching an arm to break into the scene. The steam rolled around my arm, and I slowly inched forward more, poking my head out to make sure there were no passerby around to see my popping out. The sound of passing cars and music from a nearby restaurant were a pleasant change from the ominous moans and deep grumbles of uku pacha. The singing of birds and ambient sounds of civilization soothed me into a false sense of security.

Rumba's voice suddenly thundered in my head. "Good. You have discovered you can enter kay pacha through the different realms. I believed in you, I knew you could do it."

I pulled out of kay pacha, a sluicing sound messing with my ears as the scene dissolved, my concentration flickering. Rumba sat close to me, her eyes scanning the surroundings. The constant bellows sound built its way to a scream. A ponderous thudding echoed everywhere.

"Be vigilant, child of Supay. Danger comes for you. But now you are ready. Trust yourself. Be yourself. Let the lessons you've learned from your dealings with the dead guide you."

"Thanks! But why does that sound like a warning?"

Rumba poofed away, steam coiling around where she'd been. A whisper of foreboding traveled up my arms and my neck. My hairs stood on end. I threw myself to the floor. A streak of purulent purple light shot where my shoulder had been, anchoring itself in the waterfall and making the water turn to brittle crystals, shards cracking and crumbling to a dull mauve.

A husky voice called out, "Hola mi nieta. Que gusto encontrarte de nuevo."

A shadowy figure stepped into view. The steam rolled away from him, hissing in muted whimpers. A tall man with black and purple robes walked toward me, his long graying hair tumbled over his shoulders. A mustache adorned a mouth that quivered with malice. His eyes… His eyes bore into me with all of Tia's intensity but none of her kindness. He smiled like he'd found prey.

"Cavillaca, te he estado buscando durante mucho tiempo. Dime, donde estan? Tu tía te escondió bien al fin. Pero debería haber sabido que no podría protegerte para siempre…"

"Huh?" I asked, trying to fake complete bewilderment, as if I were a gringa. I backed away, trying to escape the aura he projected with his flowing gray cape and smooth black staff. A miasma of something evil crackled around him. Uku pacha groaned around me as if he wasn't supposed to be here. His very form chittered and broke apart, only to reform violently. His face popped in and out of reality, as he continued to speak.

"No entiendes el español? You are a child of Supay. You bring dishonor to your heritage."

I stopped looking for an escape, every tunnel, every cave entrance seeming to duplicate around me anyway. From the corner of my eyes, I noticed the faint forms of the dead coming to watch us.

Child of Supay. Rumba had called me that, what seemed like so long ago. What was that? As I thought it through, my deranged uncle laughed at me.

"You don't even know what you are. Hija tonta. Why would a god choose you of all people to do his work? You call yourself a child of Supay? No matter. I have come to claim you and finish what I started fourteen years ago."

The impact of his words left me stunned. Supay. A god. My readings came back to me in full force. Supay the god of death. *That* Supay. I hadn't heard his name spoken out loud. I'd pronounced it the American way, 'sup-pay. Suddenly, everything came together and make sense, the reason the dead came to me, and why I could go to them. Me being able to access the In-Between, the pachas… The answer had been in front of me this whole time. Just like with Reggie, just like with Angelica and Niko. I needed to trust my instincts a whole lot more. My own doubt held me back.

I screamed as a mass flew at me, toppling me over. The hot ground burned my back. Falling against a stalagmite tore open my cheek. My uncle was on top of me, his robes splayed over my entire body. His fetid breath lanced me as he grabbed me by the throat.

"Silly child. Your aunt tried so hard to protect you. But I have always been the clever one. You are sloppy. You left huge imprints of your passing wherever you went. I tried to follow… but the voices… the voices told me it wasn't yet time. And your glow disappeared if I followed too long. I wondered if you didn't have a protector."

He looked around, his marzipan-colored eyes darting every which way. He shook me by the throat, my head connecting painfully with the ground.

"Where is your protector now? You're mine," he huffed, squeezing my throat tighter. I fought against him, fingers scrabbling at leather-thick skin.

He started to howl, shaking his head back and forth. He mumbled in quick succession, words and spittle flying from his mouth. His own neck began to fritter apart, and with a scream he let go of me, his entire body dislocating and squelching apart in a spray of black goo.

I inched away, fighting against the heaviness of his robes and cloak.

"My dear Cavillaca, my sister's daughter, I wouldn't–"

"Raaaaahhh! Your powers will satiate the hunger of the great Chullachaki. I should have killed you as soon as I took you…" His voice broke as it navigated between his insane psyche and the shriveled remains of his sanity.

"I'm sorry, I'm sorry, I have no choice, my mind is no longer mine–"

"Our family has suffered the curse of the gods for too long! I will show them, I will show them!"

His voice bounced back and forth between a reedy plaintive voice, and the husky growl I was more familiar with. His eyes rolled, his teeth bared, his hands clawed at the air. Glimmers of empathy shone through in his eyes when his voice changed. But I knew he was in a losing battle. I needed to escape now.

I scrabbled away, trying to find the glowing lines back to the door. My concentration wavered as my uncle continued to howl. Focus, focus! I tried to concentrate on the steamship deck, on finding my friends, but my thoughts crumbled away like my uncle's sanity.

Gasping, I whirled, trying to recognize the tunnels I'd passed. They all looked the same, craggy monoliths stretching agonizingly to the barren heavens, deep tunnels carving a trail of charnel and death of hope profoundly in the ground. If I could find a puddle of water, I could flash back to the In-Between.

I hopped away, scaring some dead who peered at me fearfully. They grabbed at me, their wispy hands *grabbing* nothing. There! In that tunnel on the left side, I glimpsed a shimmer; a puddle of water!

I screamed as something wrapped around me and yanked me backward. In my struggle, I only saw a thorny black strand wrapped tightly around my midriff.

The madman laughed, tapping his staff on the ground. "You

didn't think it would be that easy, did you?"

His magic coil sank into me, breaking my skin. My eyes watered at the pain, blood seeping out and turning black where it touched his foul magic.

"Your sacrifice will take away my broken mind. He has promised it! I will bring the best back to this family. Our family deserves greatness! We are children of the land; we have inherited the magic of the earth and skies."

I ripped at the magic coil, but my nails became purple and brittle, my fingers became numb. Shuddering, I stopped, glaring hatefully and fearfully at my crazy uncle.

"But first," he said, tapping long, yellowed nails on the top of his staff. "First I need to take what should be mine."

He yanked me backward completely, till I was at eye height with him. He grabbed my neck again and the coil around my belly vanished. He squeezed and my vision swam. My lungs screamed as he *pulled*. He gestured and hooked his fingers in the air around something inside me. A faint trail of light blossomed timidly and spooled out to him. The more he yanked, the weaker I felt. I couldn't breathe. I couldn't even whisper. Every fiber of my being wanted to shout for Rumba. She said I was ready. She was wrong.

How could I stop him? He was draining me. He was draining my power. That light… that light was the same shade as the dusky sun that had visited my bedroom for so many months now. It was mine.

He crooked his fingers and my light spun faster, unspooling and going into his body. The world started to lose color, sounds became muted. He flashed me into a memory.

He was in the rainforest, carrying me. I was a baby in his arms, wailing and crying. Mosquitoes kept flying around us, trying to dissuade us from continuing. The heavy vegetation glistened with fresh rain, he coughed and gibbered as an episode hit him.

Flash.

I was on the forest floor, still a baby, linens wrapped around me. A tall, dark-haired woman fired white sparks of magic from her hands. My uncle shot back at her, that sickly power connecting with hers and canceling both magical streams. The ground around them shook like the ripples of an earthquake. Singed leaves, crumpled vines, and sizzled fruit lay smashed and broken. The woman, my Tia, angled herself as if to hug him, then shot a full blast of white light at his chest. He toppled backward, and she rushed toward me, picking me up. Half of her hair was singed, and cuts marred her neck.

"Cavilla, my darling. You are safe now, you are safe now, I will keep you safe."

She stared at him, tears streaming down her face. "Leave us alone! I never want to see you again. Murderer of my sister. If you'd just asked for help… I might have been able to free you. Why? Why didn't you?" she asked his prone form.

Flash.

As a baby I lay against his chest, rain pouring on our faces. Frantic screams echoed through the forest. A woman dashed out of a thick clump of bushes, her hair wild, her clothing ripped to shreds. Not far behind her was a man, in similar distress, running forward.

"Put her down! Give us our daughter back, Jorge!"

My uncle stopped backing away and threw a cloud of dark sand at them. The man and woman– my parents, fell to the ground, coughing, rubbing at their eyes.

"I can't. She is my only salvation," he said sadly. He dropped me as a yowl ripped through his innards.

My mother crawled on the ground, her eyes on me. She was beautiful, her hair the same wild mess as mine, her eyes as heavy-lidded and alert as mine. From my father, I could tell I'd inherited his slight build, and his darker skin.

"We can help you, Jorge. Trust us please. Whatever deal you have made, we can help."

"You can't!" he shrieked. "A sacrifice for another! She will have the power of the gods. Give her up!"

"Jamás!" my parents yelled.

"Then I can't spare you," Jorge said.

A flat bar of magic appeared from his hands. The bar flattened them both, forcing them to gasp for air.

He flicked his wrist, and the bar became a blade. The blade sank into my parents' necks and severed their heads. At least that's what I deduced. My vantage point was skewed from my position on the ground.

I still felt like my power was being drained. But it was going more slowly. I remained trapped inside the memory of baby me. He was strong; breaking free of the memory required brute strength.

Yet, his form was breaking apart. The realization that he wasn't holding me by the throat also dawned on me. My throat relaxed, and my lungs stopped heaving. The bile at seeing him murder my parents came up, and I spewed all over the rainforest floor.

The grief, the hatred, the shock all came out in my vomit. I crawled away from my pile of sick, pushing against his mental constraints. If I could just get completely free…

The next moment, the memory shattered as he grabbed me by the throat– not the memory of him, but his actual body in the uku pacha. Again, he sucked on my power, and my light started to filter back into him. The numbness closed around me again, both around my body and my heart. His grip slackened, and his body tore in two, like clouds being parted by an angry hand, before fusing together again.

He wasn't invincible. Whatever hold he had in uku pacha was feeble. He wasn't dead. He wasn't completely alive either, maybe due to Chulluchaki's curse. Hence, I was master of this realm.

As his body slipped into the insubstantial once more, I readied myself. When his magic coil let go of me for a moment, I flopped to the ground.

Pressing my hands to the ground, I concentrated on the beating rhythm of uku pacha. It was a regular pounding now, as if invisible miners were working the earth. I focused on my own negative emotional state, connecting with the feelings of the dead I sensed around me. My rage at his murder of my parents, my sorrow at never knowing my family, my sorrow at Tia's withholding of information, my sorrow at Niko and Angelica's deaths, the realization that a neighbor kept mum to keep her nephew out of prison, the shock at realizing Reggie's killer wasn't just a killer but also a woman beater, the sorrow that my own uncle was a broken wreck of a human being; it all climaxed in a wound of raw pain. The essence of the dead huddling behind the tunnel walls, crawling around puddles, screaming their infinite dread of being stuck here, merged with my pain.

Come to me, I commanded, *and help me throw this imposter out of this realm.*

I breathed in their pain and used mine as a compass. Rage, rage, sorrow, sorrow, grief, grief, bitterness, ever more bitterness.

Feed it to him, a dark part of me whispered.

The intangible forms of the dead surged out of their crooks and crevices and crannies. They lunged forward, going where I pointed my finger. They swarmed over my uncle, their pattering feet a faint whisper of doom in this loud place.

I continued to feed my pain through the veins of earth and rock. More dead flitted out, covering my uncle in their translucent corpses. He sank under their weight, thrashing futilely. Their screams mingled with his.

His screeches soothed my heart. Let him suffer from the consequences of his actions.

Yet, I felt a tiny shift. A subtle change in the dynamics of this realm. The background beat became discordant. The dead trembled, and all at once, a dull, pulsing faded light pushed outward from the mass of the dead. It sucked at them, and the dead started to fall over, dazed. A few tumbled at my feet, eyes wide, in a nearly comatose state. I touched them and flinched. Jorge was using their power, my power. He had pain of his own, and he was using that to disrupt my punishment. That queer sensation of being hollowed out came back. I severed my flow with the dead, and they dispersed, in a flurry of whispers and lingering moans.

Jorge stood smiling at me, smoothing his robes. I flicked at him with my power, my hands still on the ground; the equivalent of putting a toe in a cold swimming pool.

I staggered as the weight of his magic slammed against mine. He'd done this before. He'd gone into the pachas before, using his dark magic and taboo knowledge of the gods, magic he wasn't supposed to have. He couldn't stay too long in these realms, but he could access them. Particularly uku pacha, as that was where he was headed once he actually died. To keep himself from dissolving, from completely caving in to Chulluchaki's curse, he went in uku pacha and siphoned out the essence of the dead. Their essence, their pain gave him strength.

I was making him stronger. But what was taken could be given back. For every action there was a reaction. And boy, was he in for a world of repercussion. Massaging my neck and wondering if I wasn't insane, I walked toward him, hands in the air. "I give in. You are so much stronger than I."

He held out his arms as if to hug me. I mimicked the gesture, readying my mind and body for what I needed to do. I would have to touch him for my plan to work. I needed some insight into how he'd pulled off his essence and power drainage. Once I had that, I could flip the tables on him.

He ensnared me in a suffocating embrace, and his magic coil wrapped around me for what I vowed would be the last time. He commenced to leech my power; I studied it, trying to tamp down the panic mounting in my head. I wrapped my arms around his lanky frame, feeling for the essence of the dead he'd drained. Ribbons of magic intertwined, going straight to his heart and brain. He was using my uncertainty to grab my power and appropriate it. To extract power from the dead, he used his own pain to overwhelm and claim theirs. I sniffed, studying harder, knowing I was on a ticking clock.

He used a knitting gesture of all things to make both drainages happen. And his concentration … his concentration relied on something close to mine, stepping sideways into reality. His power was a lot like mine, just more warped and twisted. Also, his magic rippled, like water and air. He relied on the delicate currents of those elements.

I used my memory of meeting Angelica and Niko dead for the first time, and my ensuing trips to the In-Between, to anchor my magic. I knew what my magic was based on: the earth and light. I knew it like I knew I was the master of the dead. All my uncle knew was to take and copy. What I discovered, I discovered on my own, through research, experiments, and hours of tears and headaches. *My* determination, *my* efforts were the source of my power. Not his.

I made that hooking gesture with my hand, discreetly enough so he wouldn't see it. Then I touched the coil around my neck. His feelings and magic threatened to submerge me. Memories of helping Reggie, my friends, Mr. Jackson, my arguments with Tia, gave me the strength I needed. I may not have known the full extent of my power, but I would grow into it. And I'd never claimed something that wasn't mine.

The dead were my partners. Not my slaves. They were my responsibility. I was meant to help them and keep the pachas in balance.

His magic… it was weak. I touched his coil gingerly and mimicked his gestures from earlier. I didn't want to take his power into me. I just wanted to extract it. *Come on*, I whispered to myself, rapidly unraveling his magic from me. He gasped, and the coil released around my neck. As soon as he started to topple, I pushed him to the ground.

He flailed, trying to hit me with his staff. I squirreled out of the way. I kept yanking on his magic, as he thrashed, banging his head against the floor. Better make it as quick and painless as possible. I stepped sideways into the realm already apart from reality, focusing on the half shadows and half lights that made up my power, the gritty determination of the earth. I wanted his power, and to give it back where it belonged.

With a flick of my hand, I scooped out his magic source, and sculpted it into a ball of putty that rested in my left hand. The rest of the essence that belonged to the dead, identifiable by the red-orange sparks, I flung into uku pacha, tendrils of dark magic sizzling and evaporating, morphing into a fine dust. A collective sigh erupted from everywhere, overpowering the ambient thudding of the realm.

Graciassss. A sibilant murmur seeped from the walls, from the tunnels, from the stagnant puddles.

I stared down at Jorge, his face frozen in a rictus. His body quaked, and a sheen of pale light passed over it. The curtain of light exploded, and I was sent tumbling head over heels. His magic, that I'd managed to hold, flew loose.

Shadows and echoes danced around me in a confusing stampede. I tried to lift my head and couldn't.

9

CASES MOSTLY CLOSED

I came to, via a rough tongue licking my cheek. A furry head butted against my forehead. After a few repetitions, I groaned.

"You did well, Cavilla," Rumba said, edging away as I fumbled my way upright. "So very well."

I held my hand to my head, flinching as pain radiated in my left palm. I stared at it, my head still swimming. An ugly amorphous purple mark was etched in my hand. "Jorge's magic," I cried out loud, almost retching as the movement made the room spin.

"Relax, it is still here," Rumba purred contentedly. She nodded toward a spot on my left. Craning my head with difficulty, I noticed his ball of magic floating as a mass defying gravity amid the lurid warm tones of uku pacha. She glanced at my hand. "It is only a temporary mark. You managed to extract his magic without letting it taint you."

Gracias a Dios. There was so much left to do. And currently, neither my head nor my body wanted to do anything.

Rumba asked, "What were you thinking of doing with his magic?"

"I want his magic given to Chulluchaki, to settle any remaining debt."

With a start, I noticed my uncle's body still lay there, inert.

Rumba smiled, a hint of the deity that resided within her curling her lips and exposing her fangs.

"Excellent idea. I will assist. I know your battle has left you weak. I think your magic was felt across all realms; that last explosion was you."

Rumba pushed me to sit up and she morphed into her true form. A vague figure shimmered into existence, an immensely tall muscular man with two snakes sprouting from his head, mismatched eyes, and fangs jutting over bearded lips. Ai-Apaec chuckled and somehow transported me to a cascade, a mirror into kay pacha. His long furry mustache dangled past his fangs, tickling my face.

"Chulluchaki! The child of Supay has a gift for you!" He/she called out.

We leapt through, though I wondered if I was delirious. Jungle sounds surrounded us. The joyful gurgle of an actual cascade quickly gave way to the roaring of a panther walking toward us. Except one moment it was a sleek black panther, the next it was a short, rotund man clothed in rags with mismatched feet. He hobbled over to us, his protuberant eyes going from Rumba to me. Rumba put me down.

"Ai-Apaec? Long time no see. Is that an heir to the Eugenio Ramirez family? They have a debt they owe me. Is she going to be my offering?"

Rumba/Ai Apaec loomed over me protectively. I was still sitting up, though only just. My head spun more violently.

"Tell him what you told me," Rumba said gently. *Strength, courage*, she telegraphed through her calm gaze.

My teeth chattered, fearful of facing the demon "I… I ran into my uncle Jorge. He tried to drain my power. I actually drained his. He stole from the dead. The cycle of ill luck my family has… It has to stop. I am offering his power in exchange for leaving us alone."

Chulluchaki swiveled his head toward the ball of Jorge's magic that floated in the air near us.

"Your mark is all over it," he hissed. "Your family has dabbled in forbidden arts. You have brought the ire of the gods. This Jorge owed me a tremendous debt for defacing my forest. You… you are special. You jest not, Ai-Apaec. She truly is a child of Supay."

Rumba nodded. Chulluchaki smiled.

"Well done. I consider any debt settled." He took the ball of magic and swallowed it whole. A tremor followed in the forest as he did so.

"You are the heir of Supay himself. Any debt is with him

anyway. You will stay eternal. As long as you serve him, and help with the dead, help maintain balance between the pachas, the curse on your family will be lifted. You are people of the earth. Your affinity will always be deeply linked with the world of the gods."

Rumba glanced at me, as I toppled forward. The damp forest floor smushed against my cheek.

"She is weakened from her battle," Rumba said. I will take her back for healing." To me, she said, "We will talk more about your responsibilities later."

Ai-Apaec scooped me in his arms, and my head lolled. He didn't look so bad in his godly form.

"Ah one more thing," Chulluchaki said, "I want the dark magic wielder's physical body and soul. He is mine."

"By all means," Ai-Apaec said.

He reached out a foot into uku pacha and tossed the body over to the forest creature. A last thought worked its way into my consciousness. Jorge's soul would never go into the pachas. He would be completely erased from existence, from meta existence. He had made his choice. A twinge of sorrow at what it had come to shuddered through me before I passed out in Rumba's arms.

***

It took a couple weeks for me to regain full strength. I even missed school. Tia was frantic. But her panic turned into astonishment when Rumba appeared and manifested in her Ai-Apaec form. I thought Tia was going to faint from shock. The god explained everything to her. As did I. It felt like a massive weight was coming off my chest at last. When we'd finished our story, Tia was white as the sheets, but a proud smile graced her features, amid the tears she'd shed.

"Mi hija, haciendo el trabajo de los dios…" she whispered almost in awe.

She hugged me hard and so did I. We didn't talk after that initial conversation. She let me rest.

Angelica and Niko came to visit. They high fived me. Only when I felt better did I tell them what I'd learned about their deaths. They looked at each other, frowns on both their faces.

"What do you want me to do?" I asked, sitting on my bed while they sat cross-legged at the end.

Angie spoke slowly. "I feel like he should go to jail. Who knows how many more people he'll hurt?"

Niko shook his head. "He might, even if Cavilla doesn't out him. It sucks. But what does going to jail do? We're still dead."

Angelica sighed. "If he continues to be a drunk driver, he might kill more people."

"Yes, but Angie, it's no longer our business. Think! We can move on. We'll finally be able to move on. We can go to that cool hanan pacha place Cavilla keeps talking about. And stay there. No more wandering about."

I nodded but kept quiet. This was their choice.

Angelica tried to twist the bed sheets and failed. "I guess that's good. I mean, all we really wanted to know was the name. We know who did it. And he didn't do it on purpose. If he had, I would want to haunt him." She laughed. "It's not worth staying stuck here though. Yes, Niko, let's move on."

He smiled. They angled in for a group hug. I hugged them back, feeling them dissolve in a shower of dusky light.

I held in my tears, both joyful and sad. They would move on. But it wasn't goodbye forever. I would see them in hanan pacha. Just as I would be able to see Mr. Jackson. I had only ventured into hanan pacha the one time. But I had a feeling I would see a whole lot more of it soon.

***

As ever, the world of the living and the dead didn't stop moving on. When I finally felt better, I went back to school, just in time to finish the semester before the winter holidays.

I had some unfinished business of my own. Angie and Niko felt fine moving on, and I'd soon confirm with them in person once I had the strength to go into hanan pacha. But I didn't feel fine just letting Mrs. Peloza's nephew continue with his bad life habits.

Hence, there I was, having been dropped off from school and walking straight from the bus stop to her house. Her nephew's car was parked in the open garage. I checked the recycle bin. It was full of nothing but alcoholic bottles. I knocked on the door. I sensed movement on the other side, but no one opened or responded. I got a flash of her stooped behind the door, her eyes squeezed shut, her hair flopping from a messy bun.

"Look Mrs. Peloza. It is I, Cavilla. Obviously, Nicholas hasn't changed his habits. I can see that. My friends have moved on. I have not. Your nephew can hurt more people. He will continue if he doesn't stop. One day, I'm going to be a private investigator. I would hate to have to bring him to justice because he killed more of my friends or even strangers. Even if he doesn't kill intentionally, he is old enough to know the consequences of his actions. This has to stop. You have to stop letting him do this. So, I have an ultimatum." I was proud of myself. My words came out strong and steady, my stomach resolute, not doing flip flops. "Either you talk with Nicholas and force him to change. Maybe go to AA meetings or something. If he doesn't listen, threaten him with jailtime, that you *will* go to the police. Or I will tell what I know to Angie and Niko's parents. I won't go to the police. That is not my job yet. Plus, the only real evidence is your testimony. Yet, I hope your conscience will choose what's right. We all need closure."

I stopped, waiting for her to answer. When she didn't, I shifted and adjusted my backpack, walking away. "I will keep an eye on you, and see if you do the right thing," I called out.

I walked past several children from other neighborhoods, coming to visit their friends. I hoped they would never cross Nicholas's path, and continue to live long, carefree lives.

***

When I no longer felt dizzy, I called on my power to access the In-Between. I ventured into kay pacha through uku pacha to spy on Bob Twindlo. It took a few tries to get it right. I ruffled around in the town of Bloomington, until I memorized his patterns, his house. I shamelessly pulled a Reggie and stalked him, hiding behind trees and bushes, noting his habits in my notebook.

It took weeks of methodically dipping into kay pacha, and searching his house, to get closer to what I needed. One day, I managed to sneak inside his basement. It was full of gym equipment and sports apparel. Duffel bags overflowing with equipment sat, gaping open like wounds. I opened each of them, and rifled through, keenly aware of the amount of time I had. Some of the bags had a lone weight, with random items in the bag; a watch here, or a bracelet there. I couldn't make sense of it.

A few weeks later, I hit the jackpot. I watched Bob saunter in his basement and open a closet. He opened a secret panel inside and took out some duffel bags. I kept in a shout of surprise. Some of the bags I had searched had gone missing or been moved. Now I knew where they'd gone.

He opened one bag and stroked some weights, chuckling to himself. He slipped in a silk pink scarf. "Too easy. Just like that Lauren and her daughter. They never put up a fight."

He closed the closet door and walked upstairs. I waited till his footsteps were firmly above me and stepped into kay pacha fully. My legs shook. Holding the portal slightly open but not entering took a toll.

I went immediately to the panel and took out the duffel bags. Each was full of weights, some had minor dents in them. But mostly the random objects I'd detected in previous searches made sense. They were trophies. From his victims. Judging from the feminine items, his victims were all girls or women. I counted. There were six bags total.

I sat back on my haunches, my guts churning. How many people exactly had he killed?

Would I ever get proof he'd killed Reggie? Reggie had been smothered. There wouldn't be a duffel bag for that. The murder weapon had been a pillow.

I could try to bring a recording device and observe him going through his bags. Perhaps he'd incriminate himself. But the proof would be thrown out in court. Everyone would wonder where it had come from.

Grimacing, I opted for a sloppy, cliché solution. I took out the bags, making sure my hands left no trace. (I wore gloves, but one could never be too careful—even though I was sure my power cloaked my presence and touch). I left them on his air hockey table. Then I made a call from inside his house, claiming someone was in danger and was being held captive in the basement.

By the end of the day, Bob had been taken into police custody.

***

The police had chatted with Bob in the basement and almost let him go until he freaked out and noticed the bags sitting on the table. Naturally, the bags were taken and investigated, bringing the truth to light. He had been murdering women. His favorite method—beating them to death. All the items matched up to his victims. I missed the interrogations as I searched for Reggie.

Reggie refused to move on. He wanted to stick around until justice was meted out. I warned him it might take a few years. He didn't mind. Penance for how he treated Dalea, he said. Shocked, I wondered when exactly in the course of events that Reggie had grown up.

10

HEART TO HEART

During winter break, I sat Tia down as she was making coquito. The kitchen smelled of coconut, and her hads dripped from milk, but I asked her about our family again. I told her about my theory, that I thought I could visit the living members of our family through hanan pacha.

Her hands trembled, and she wiped her face, smearing her hair and cheeks with milk. She laughed, but there were tears too.

"Hija. I will never understand what you do. But you are a child of a god. All I can do is support you. I warn you though, if you do intend on visiting them, you are in for a long, long trip. We are many. I'm sure our family has expanded since I was last in touch with them all those years ago. Our family has always been prolific." She chuckled.

She took a breath and poured coquito into intricate glass bottles. She washed her hands and snipped some holiday-themed ribbons, wrapping them around the neck of the bottles. She went to the attic and returned with a hot glue gun. Tia plugged it in, and as it heated, she smiled at me.

"So, what are the names that I saw in the letters?" I asked. "Are those people still alive?"

She shook her head. "Most of them have passed away. Manuela, Jose, Eduardo, Gloria, Pablo, Camilla, and Dolores were your grandparents. My mom was Gloria. I think only Eduardo, Manuela and Pablo are alive. But that was before we moved here. For all I know, they died in the meantime." Her shoulders slumped.

"I will find out," I vowed. "Don't worry."

She straightened, wiping a few stray tears.

"Didn't you mention something about seventeen great-grandparents?"

"Yes," she said, testing the glue gun and hissing as it burned. "We do. They are all dead. But they were numerous and practically held up the village by themselves! Their names were Francesca, Hilda, Alejandro, Chichi, Bela, Mateo, Santiago, Emmanuel, Felipe, Angela, Natalia, Vera, Ariana, Sergio, Diego, Lucas, and Maia. I remember most of them. All the kindest people you could ever have met. They had the grandest parties. They helped everyone they knew. Some of them had children out of wedlock. There are plenty of descendants of ours running around. I'm sure you have cousins, second cousins, third cousins and more populating Peru at this point. I don't know them though."

My head spun. So many people. I would never be able to keep them straight in my head. "We come from Ollantaytambo, right?"

Tia nodded. "Though most of us moved to Chinchero. My generation and my cousin's generations wanted a fresh start. But we come from the Andes. The Andes is our ancestral home. We have Portuguese blood too. The conquistadors came and mingled with us. That is why I suspect our brujeria has been diluted. Why we are fairer-skinned than we ever used to be. Though, blood must not matter that much, as you are the child of Supay."

A lump in my throat formed as she said that so calmly, so kindly. No judgment.

"Now we are scattered everywhere. I know some of my cousins are in Europe as well. Victoria, Emilia, Elias, and Joaquin… There are more. So many more. Hija, you will spend a lifetime finding family."

She took a Christmas ornament and glued it to the bottle. When she turned, her face was awash with tears.

"It feels so good to say their names. Having to withhold it all was like forcing an abyss within me. It is strange to know I can say all this… without fear."

I squirmed in my seat. "Are you sure you don't hate me because I had to kill your brother? I mean, I didn't really kill him.

Technically Chulluchaki did that, but—"

She waved a hand. "You did what you had to. You did what I didn't have the courage to do. You are stronger than I ever was. It is fitting you have a godlike power. Truly, you bring balance to the spirit world and to our own family."

She paused. "I hate what he became. I hate that killing him was inevitable. I mostly hate you had to finish what I couldn't. But no hija, I could never hate you."

She let go of the ornament to hug me hard. The ornament fell to the ground, dried glue exposed to the air.

The rest of the conversation lapsed into more calming waters. I took out my parchment paper with the sad beginnings of a family tree. She gave me name after name and dates, though I had to scratch out a few as her memory faltered. She talked about old memories of her immediate family—parties, escapades, and hunts, going into the mountains and looking at the stars. By the time we were done, the coquito was almost warm.

Tia put the bottles in the fridge and said, "Mrs. Peloza must have gone out of retirement. Her car is gone most of the day. I also see a young man with her. Is he a new beau?"

I laughed. "No. Surely, it's her nephew."

Tia shrugged. "The other day I saw her yelling at him to get in the car and let her drive. He didn't seem happy at all, but he went. I wonder where they were going…"

I smiled but said nothing. It didn't involve Tia. It seemed Mrs. Peloza was growing a spine after all.

I truly would have wanted Tia to witness me doing my magic, but I knew she wouldn't be able to see it. I could have taken her to our other family members. Alas, I'd have to find another way for that to happen.

"Cavilla, help me make these cookies," she said gesturing to bags of flour, cornstarch, powdered sugar, cinnamon sticks, and canned dulce de leche.

I squealed. "We're making alfajores?"

She nodded.

Even work with the dead vanished from my mind as we happily worked on the cookies well into the evening.

***

I teetered on the edge of a window into kay pacha, having followed the lines that glowed, thanks to the family letters I had brought with me. The soothing serenity of hanan pacha, the burble of birds, the scent of Spanish moss and citronella passed over me. In the mirror to the real world, I saw a family of dark-haired people bustling about, working. They all had my genes. This was a part of my family. Two halves of my heart burned softly. My parents had guided me here. I felt it. Now, they led me to their remaining kin, for a family's soul is never truly lost. It is passed in the generations throughout time. I knew these peoples' names. But they didn't know me. I knew it wouldn't be a problem.

My work has only just begun, and so had my family's redemption.